Honor and Obey

By

Teresa Mummert

Copyright

Chapter One

My thoughts were spinning out of control and I gripped William's hands tightly in mine until the skin of my knuckles turned white.

"Marry me," William repeated, his eyes burning into mine. My words caught in my throat and I suddenly had the urge to flee.

"What if...what if someone found out? What if you lose your job?" My voice was panicked and I was practically yelling. He placed his hand on my cheek and stroked it soothingly. I closed my eyes, trying to calm myself down.

"I don't care about any of that anymore, but even if I did, you're not my student anymore. When I almost lost you, I realized what was important to me. I don't ever want you to leave my side again." He pressed his lips against mine, begging me to say yes. I got lost in his touch for a moment but quickly regained composure.

"I can't ask you to do that," I said, placing my hand on his chest. His heart was beating wildly. His muscles flexed under his jaw.

"You didn't ask," he replied, his words sharp and I could tell he was on the verge of losing his patience.

"I'm not saying no." My voice was barely a whisper. I wanted so badly to jump in his arms and scream yes from the top of my lungs but I couldn't be the reason he lost everything in his life. I knew his father hated me and make his life miserable.

He would eventually regret it and in turn, he would regret me. His body pulled back from mine. I put my hands on either side of his face and stared him directly in the eye. "I want to marry you. I just need some time. Take things

2

slow," I said, forcing a small smile. William's hands met mine and he squeezed them gently.

"That's all I want," he said, wrapping his arms around me and spinning me around. I couldn't help but let myself get lost in his happiness. I squeezed his neck tightly and buried my face in his chest, breathing in his musky scent. When I thought about all we had been through; the ex-wife, the jealous girlfriend, the even more jealous husband of said girlfriend and the horrible way William's father had treated us, I couldn't even begin to imagine how others would take the news of us being married. I wanted to run away with him. I wanted to forget about Florida and all of the trouble that had come along so far and just get lost with him, but I knew that was impossible. Even with all of the money in the world, and William did possess quite a bit, we could never hide from everyone forever. His family would find out—and probably cut him off. William kissed me softly, lingering just above my mouth, leaving me craving more. The mood around us shifted from panic and excitement to pure lust. I slipped my fingers up his neck into his hair. His hand twisted into a knot in my hair, tugging gently.

"Never leave me, Emma," he whispered.

"Never," I replied. His mouth found mine, hard. His tongue pushed gently against my lips and I let them fall open for him. His other hand slid down my spine and over my bottom, squeezing gently. I let out a quiet moan into his mouth. His hand moved further down my thigh and rested below my knee. He pulled my leg up to his side as his breathing became heavier. I wanted more than anything to feel his flesh against mine, to rid my thoughts of all that we had endured. I tugged feverishly at his belt as my body ached for him. I cried out as he pushed the length of himself into my thigh.

"I want you." I breathed heavily as dampness pooled between my legs. He shoved me back onto the couch and quickly undid his shirt. I was completely caught up in the moment, sliding my hand down my thigh towards my most sensitive areas. His eyes burned with wanting as he threw his shirt to the ground and quickly undid his belt and slipped his jeans down his legs.

"Take your clothes off." His voice was low and his eyes traveled down my body as he spoke. I bit my lip and slipped my t-shirt over my head, revealing my bare swollen breasts. His jaw clenched and I continued, pulling off my shorts and panties as I lay back on the couch. I rested my hand just below my belly, running my fingertips over my skin. "Show me how badly you want me."

His words sent a shiver down my spine and my fingers automatically responded to the seductive sound of his voice. I slipped my hand lower, my fingers gliding effortlessly across my wetness. I let out a breath as I felt my insides tighten. William's hand mirrored mine as he slowly stroked himself.

"You are so beautiful."

With his words, I became bolder, dipping a finger inside myself, my back arching in response.

"Oh, god," I panted as he lowered himself onto the couch.

"Don't stop," he instructed as he traced the entrance of me with his hardness. I began to rub harder as he slipped the tip of himself inside, causing all of my muscles to tighten in response. I wanted him inside of me, deep inside of me, and I was willing to do anything he asked. His fingers found mine and he slowed my movements, making my hand move in smaller, more deliberate circles. He rocked his hips slightly, just enough to tease my body. I let my free hand slide over my breast, my nipple hardening under my fingers the way he had made it do before. I pinched it gently, as his eyes wandered over my body. My hips rocked against my hand and I was struggling to control my breathing.

"Does that feel good?" he asked, and I could barely find my voice to answer. I nodded, my lips parted.

He slipped himself in a little further and my body reacted, grabbing him and trying desperately to pull him deeper inside of me. I raised my hips, silently begging him to slide in deeper but he held firm. "That is enough of that." He grabbed my wrists and pushed them over my head. I lifted my hips again, desperate to find my release. He responded by pulling out of me completely. He repositioned himself so that he held both of my hands in one of his and slipped the other down between my legs. He slowly dragged the tip of his finger up and down, barely touching my skin.

"William, please," I cried out, tugging against his hand. He dipped a finger inside of me suddenly, nearly sending me over the edge. His mouth just inches from mine as I panted. "Please" I moaned and he slipped a second finger inside, angling just right to touch places inside of me that I didn't even know existed. I rocked against his hand, unable to stop myself. I widened my legs, making sure he could have a clear view of what he was missing. He took his thumb and slowly circled over my most sweet spot as his fingers continued to slide in and out of me. "Oh, god!" I turned my head, pressing it against the cushion.

"Look at me." His breath tickled my ear. I turned to look him in the eye, breathing in his sweet minty breath. "You wanted to take things slow."

I bucked against him with my hips out of frustration. I hadn't said no to his proposal; I just needed more time to process everything we had been through.

"You're punishing me?" I couldn't hide the anger in my voice. I wanted to slap him, and might have if he didn't have my hands pinned down. A smile crept across his face.

"I'm just doing as you asked. You have more control than you realize, Emma." His fingers slowly began to move again. I wanted to be mad at him but my body betrayed me. My hips rocked against his hand. His smile grew wider as he licked his lips and leaned closer. His breath was warm against my ear and sent a shiver throughout my body. "I only want to please you, Emma." His lips brushed along my neck.

"Then fuck me," I panted as my core tightened around him. He withdrew his fingers and shoved himself inside of me forcefully. I moaned into his ear as his grip on my hands tightened with each thrust. I wrapped my legs around him, giving him deeper access.

"I want every part of you, Emma," he panted.

"I'm yours, William."

We exploded together, our bodies becoming one for a brief moment in time. He collapsed heavily on top of my and he released my wrists. He put his hands on either side of me to push himself off the couch. I wrapped my hands around his neck and pulled him back into me.

"Please don't go." His body tensed for a moment but he did not pull against me. I knew I was asking a lot from him. All of these feelings were just as new to him as they were to me. He relaxed back onto me and pushed my hair out of my face with his fingers.

"I don't think I could leave you if I tried." He put his forehead against mine and let out a heavy breath. I let my fingers slip into his hair.

It was frightening how quickly I had fallen for William. He consumed me. It didn't matter if he was good for me anymore. It only mattered that I was with him.

We spent the rest of the night entangled in each other. As the sun rose, I tried to unwrap our bodies so I could make a fresh pot of coffee. William's arms tightened around me like a snake, holding me firmly in place.

"Don't leave me," he mumbled into my chest.

"I'm not leaving you. I just want to make some coffee," I whispered as I pushed against him.

"You will." From the tone of his voice, it was obvious he was lost in a nightmare. I stopped struggling and kissed the top of his head. I rubbed his back and waited for him to awaken. When he did, he seemed oblivious to the earlier conversation. It was hard to imagine someone like William feeling like he had no control.

Teresa Mummert

Chapter Two

William rubbed the sleep from his eyes and smiled as he glanced down at me. He had awakened in a great mood judging by the length of him pressed firmly against my inner thigh.

"It's hard to imagine I am not dreaming." He gave me a quick peck on the lips. It was an innocent gesture, but he lingered and the air around us grew thick with desire.

"If we don't get off this couch soon, we may die of starvation," I joked.

He laughed, his whole body gyrating against me in response. "You're right. I haven't eaten in a while." His eyes narrowed as he slid himself down the length of my body, leaving a trail of kisses along the way. My hands ran through his hair as my back arched towards him.

"William," I giggled. "We need to get ready for the day."

"Why?" he asked as he nuzzled my inner thigh. It tickled and I squirmed against him.

"I want you to meet my family."

His head shot up and his eyes locked onto mine.

"I thought you didn't want anyone to know about us?"

"I don't think my aunt would tell anyone. Besides, she doesn't have to know who your father is." If William wanted to take a big step like marriage, it was only right that he meet my family first. I only wish he could have met my parents, although they may not have approved of our relationship.

William slid back up the length of my body and rubbed my cheek with the pad of his thumb.

"I'll do whatever it takes to be with you."

I wrapped my arms around his neck and squeezed him tightly. His hands tangled in my hair as we lay in each other's arms. I could see us doing this every day for the rest of our lives. He had become my obsession. My every thought. I needed him to feel whole. Everything in my life before him was filled with loneliness.

Part of me wanted to introduce him to Judy to show her I was worthy of happiness. Worthy of someone's love. She should have been the person I ran to when I was feeling lonely, but she pushed me away. She was uncaring and cold. Unable to show love to me.

William was different. His world revolved around mine. I still couldn't understand his affection for me. No one had ever looked at me the way he does. Never touched me the way he does. He was intense and overwhelming, but he was mine and I was his. I loved that feeling of belonging to someone.

I felt safe with him even in the midst of all the chaos that swarmed our relationship. No matter how dominating and controlling he appeared from the outside, I knew better. He was scared to feel, scared to love, and scared to lose.

I'd be lying if I said I wasn't terrified to introduce him to my aunt. She was judgmental and distant. Regardless of how she responded, she would know that I was worthy of someone's love. I need him and I needed her to know that I didn't need her.

I expected William to be more resistant to the idea of meeting her. I had hoped for it. Going through with this would not only put her in her place, but it would make all of this that I had with William real. I'm not sure which part of that scared me more.

Teresa Mummert

"Take a nice hot shower. I'll cook us some breakfast." William kissed me gently on the forehead and smiled before pushing up onto his elbows and sliding off the couch. I stretched like a cat before taking his hand and allowing him to lift me to my feet.

I suddenly became aware at how naked I was, and wrapped my arms over my chest. William's eyes raked over the length of my body before grabbing my arm and pulling it away from my breasts.

"Don't hide yourself from me."

I reluctantly let my hands fall to my sides. I chewed on my lip as my eyes danced over his naked form. He placed his fingers under my chin and tilted my face up to meet his gaze.

"You are perfect."

My face heated with a blush as I tried to fight back a smile. What had I done to deserve him? He leaned closer, running his lips along my

17

neck up to my ear. I let out a sigh and closed my eyes, letting my head roll to the side to give him better access.

"Go take your shower before I take you into the bedroom and we don't get anything done today," he whispered in my ear. I nodded and he smacked me lightly across the bottom as I turned towards the bathroom. I looked over my shoulder and smiled at him before making my way to the other side of the room.

The water was hot and felt incredible against my skin. I washed myself twice, lingering in the warmth as long as I could. All of the stress of taking William to meet my aunt washed away. I thought again about my parents, and what they would have said if I'd brought home someone like William.

Part of me was relieved he had never pressed the issue about them, but part of me wondered why he didn't want to know about my past. Maybe it was because his was too painful.

It took us nearly losing each other before he was able to open up and tell me the truth about Abby. I know it was incredibly hard for him. Maybe he was just trying to spare me the pain. It wasn't a topic I enjoyed reliving, but I wanted to share that part of me with William. I wanted to know everything about him. He must feel the same way.

I turned off the water and grabbed the oversized white towel that hung on a rack beside the shower. I ran it over my body and secured it around myself before stepping out into the main living area.

The apartment was filled with the smell of pancakes. I smiled as I caught sight of William standing in front of the stove, dishing the last few flapjacks onto a plate on the island.

"I thought I was going to have to come in there after you." He winked and I couldn't contain my smile.

"I couldn't help myself. It felt so good." I took a seat at the island as he placed a stack of pancakes on a plate in front of me.

"You even make a shower sound sexy," he joked as he rounded the corner and took a seat next to me.

"This looks amazing!" I cut up my stack of pancakes and reached for the syrup. William's hand shot up and pushed it away. I gave him a frustrated glare and reached for it again. He slid it further down the counter and smirked in my direction.

"Careful. Remember what happened with the sugar." His eyes narrowed and I couldn't help but let out a giggle.

"I'll have to remember that for later. We have too much to do today." I wanted to get this meeting with Judy over with before I lost my nerve.

"I'm sorry, Emma. I'm going to have to meet your aunt some other time."

I slumped back into my seat and sat my fork down on my plate, trying unsuccessfully not to pout. William reached over and tucked my damp hair behind my ear.

"I got a call from my lawyer while you were in the shower. He needs me to look over some paperwork about the Abby incident. It shouldn't take long, but I think it would be best if we rescheduled the meeting for another day."

I wasn't mad at William, but I knew if we waited, I would lose my nerve. Introducing him to Judy was a huge step for our relationship. I knew he understood that. He was the one who had asked me to marry him.

He placed his fingers under my chin and angled my face towards him. "You're not mad at me, are you?"

I shook my head and smiled. "Of course not. You take care of what you have to do so we don't have to worry about Abby anymore."

He nodded once and turned his attention back to his food. "Eat."

I watched him take a few bites before picking up my fork. We ate in silence. I didn't mind because I was too busy shoving food into my mouth. William was an amazing cook. One of his many talents.

Chapter Three

William washed our plates as I retreated to his bedroom to get dressed. I pulled on my favorite pair of ripped jeans and a white tank top. I grabbed a brush from my purse was running it through my hair when I heard the door squeak open behind me. William stood in the doorway leaning against the frame. His eyes raked over my body and I felt my face flush.

"What?" I asked with a grin as he slowly walked towards me. He stopped just inches from me, his hand reaching out and tracing my jaw.

"I don't deserve you." His eyes searched mine and I couldn't help but smile. His hand slipped into my wet hair and pulled my face closer to his. Our lips brushed against each other's.

I sucked in a quick breath, the anticipation of touching him grew overwhelming. I leaned forward and kissed him quickly. His fingers knotted in my hair as he moaned into my mouth. My body sagged against his as I parted my lips and let him explore my mouth further.

His kisses were hungry, and I could feel my lips swelling as his kisses became more demanding. His free hand slipped down my back, trailing along my spine until they reached the waist of my jeans.

He pulled back, resting his forehead against mine, catching his breath.

"I have to go. I'll be back as soon as I can."

I nodded my head against his, my eyes closed, as I tried to recover from his touch. He pulled back slightly and traced my bottom lip with his thumb.

"I love you, Emma." His eyes burned into mine and his words had a direct connection to every part of my body.

"I love you, William." His lips crushed into mine hard. His hand crabbed my ass and pulled me tightly against him. A moan escaped my lips as I felt just how badly he wanted me.

"Do you have to leave now?" I asked, my eyes glancing up to the ceiling. He smiled devilishly, obviously contemplating taking me to the third floor.

"I have to do this now. I promise you, we have all the time in the world." His forehead fell back against mine as we both took a minute to steady our breathing. His tongue shot out and swiped across his bottom lip. I nearly melted in his arms. "I won't be long."

I nodded again and swallowed back my desire.

He kissed me quickly on the cheek and left the bedroom. A moment later, the front door opened and closed, the lock clicking into place behind him.

I missed him already.

I made my way into the living room and plopped down on the couch, running my hand over the cushions and smiling. I couldn't keep the dirty thoughts of last night's events out of my mind. I sighed and relaxed my head against the cushion. It was getting harder and harder to be away from him. I finally felt like myself.

After my parents died, I never thought I would feel happiness again. I pushed the thought from my mind. I had someone to share my life with now. I smiled at the idea of William meeting my aunt. My stomach was full of butterflies. It didn't matter to me what she thought of him, though. I was ready to move on with my life.

I grabbed the remote and clicked on the television. I flicked through the channels absentmindedly, settling on an old movie. It was just background noise. My thoughts were consumed by William.

I wanted to know everything about him. I wanted to know what made him smile before Abby had crushed his spirit. I wanted to know everything. I decided to lie down on the couch and let my eyes glaze over as I watched the television.

The sound of the lock turning startled me and I sat straight up, yawning as I stretched. How long had I been asleep?

William slipped inside and locked the door behind him. His eyes caught mine and he smiled slightly. He tossed a stack of papers from his lawyer onto the table. I stood and made my way around the couch towards him.

He took three large strides and his body was against mine. His arms wove around my waist and he lifted me effortlessly against him. My lips found his hungrily. He turned and planted my back hard against the wall, pulling my legs around his hips. I panted in between kisses as his body pushed against mine.

I ached for his touch. My body craved him like a drug. His fingers dug into my sides and I almost squealed in pain. His hips rotated against me again and the only sound that left me was a moan of pure pleasure. I tossed my head back against the wall and dug my fingers into his muscular shoulders. His lips trailed down my throat hungrily.

"Tell me you want me, Emma." His mouth never stopped moving against my skin.

"Ohh... I want you." I panted as he pushed against me again, moaning as he did. His hand slipped under my shirt and skimmed along my breast. I arched my back approvingly. He was being rough, but I'd be lying if I said his aggressive nature didn't turn me on. There was something dangerous about William that made him irresistible. His lips found their way to mine again and he released me, his fingers worked quickly to undo my jeans. He slipped them down over my hips as I wiggled to free myself from them. I reached for his belt to undress him, but he grabbed my hands, pushing them above my head. I bucked my hips out toward him, but he moved, not letting me make the connection. His mouth hovered over mine. His lips grazed my cheek as they made their way to my ear. He nibbled gently on my earlobe. My body was set on fire.

"Please!" I begged. I wanted him against me. My body ached for him to be inside of me. I felt his lips curl into a smile.

"I love it when you beg." His voice was husky and full of lust.

"Please," I whispered, letting my eyes flutter closed. His hips found mine again.

He pulled back from me slightly. His eyes grew serious.

"I would do anything for you... anything."

I didn't process a coherent thought. I just needed to feel him against me, inside me. I nodded quickly and his mouth found mine. He grabbed my shirt and pulled it over my head in one quick motion. I stood in front of him in only my yellow cotton panties. A growl resonated from deep in his chest. It was so erotic and primal. I began to fumble with the buttons on his shirt, wanting to see his body. He didn't push my hands away, only smirked slightly as he watched me work. I knew it took a lot for him to give up any of the control.

I avoided his gaze as I concentrated on getting him as naked as possible. As I reached the final button I pushed the shirt off his shoulders, exposing his deep tribal tattoo that wound its way over his shoulder and down his arm. His eyes danced over my body and I bit my lip, waiting for him to make a move. He grinned and lifted my body against his. He pulled my legs around his waist and I held onto him as he made his way to the bedroom.

His hands frantically searched my body as he tasted the skin above my breast. I arched my back, pressing myself into him. He moaned and made quick work of undoing his belt. I let my nails slide down his back, feeling his muscles flex under my fingertips.

"I want you, Emma. I want to possess you," he groaned. I whimpered at his confession. It made me want him even more. He slipped his jeans over his hips, not bothering to remove them the rest of the way. "Tell me that you're mine."

"Ahhh…" was all that I could mutter. His lips on my body felt too incredible. His hand slipped up my throat to my jaw and he jerked my face to his.

"Tell me!" His words were threatening. He ground his hips into mine.

"I'm yours. Only yours," I panted. His eyes widened and his fingers slipped between us. He wrapped his fingers in my panties and tugged them, ripping the small scrap of fabric from my body. My hips lifted as I rubbed myself against his hardness. Pleasure shot through me all the way to my toes.

He wrapped his hand around himself and rubbed the tip of him at my entrance.

"Ahhh…" My voice shook as I gripped onto the blanket beside me, my head falling back.

"Look at me. I want to watch you come." His words alone caused my hips to buck. My eyes met his as he slowly pressed against my entrance, slipping inside, painfully slow. My mouth hung open as I struggled to breathe.

His finger slid over my wetness before coming up to my mouth. He ran his moist finger over my bottom lip. His hips held perfectly still. My tongue darted out, licking the tip.

He moaned and shoved forward, burying himself deep inside of me. I bit my lip to keep from crying out in pleasure as I rocked my hips to keep up with his fast and powerful thrusts. He grunted as he pounded into me over and over.

"I… love… you…" he said through gritted teeth.

I squeezed my thighs against his hips.

"I love you!" I cried as I squeezed the blanket tightly in my fingers. My words were his undoing. He slammed into me two more times as he spilled his seed inside me. My body jerked as my insides clenched him tightly. My own orgasm rippled through my body. His hips continued to rock until every last drop of pleasure had passed through me.

His body relaxed heavily on mine as I finally let go of the bed and laced my fingers behind his neck.

We lay together, our bodies still connected, until our breathing slowed back to normal. His head was buried in the crook of my neck.

"I love you," I whispered in his ear. I felt him twitch inside of me. I smiled. He kissed lightly up my neck until he reached my ear.

"I love you so much, Emma."

I squeezed my arms tightly around him. We drifted off to sleep wrapped in each other's arms. Life was perfect.

Chapter Four

My hands shot out beside me, reaching for William, but they came up empty. I rubbed the sleep from my eyes and yawned, stretching like a cat. I finally blinked my eyes open and glanced around. I was alone. My heart sank for a moment. Small noises came from the kitchen and a grin spread over my face. I slipped off the bed and searched the room. I grabbed a small torn piece of yellow fabric and smiled. I dropped the panties and rummaged through my suitcase for something to wear. I grabbed a tank and a pair of jeans and began to dress.

I couldn't wait to lay eyes on William, the man I loved. I opened the bedroom door and inhaled the wonderful scent of coffee. His eyes met mine. He was shirtless, his jeans hanging low on his hips, belt hanging.

"Sleep well?" he asked.

I grinned from ear to ear and nodded my head as I walked quickly towards him. He held out his arms for me, and I wrapped mine around his neck as he lifted me in a tight embrace.

"Shame. I was going to say if you weren't happy, we could try again." He winked, lowering me so my toes touched the ground. I smacked him playfully on the chest and his arm grabbed my wrist. His eyes burned with fire. I chewed on my lip as I looked up at him.

"Careful. You know I like to play rough." He smirked and released my hand. I felt a blush creep across my face. He turned back to the counter and grabbed a mug, holding it out for me. A fresh cup of coffee, cream and sugar included.

"Thanks." I inhaled, closing my eyes. I sighed and let my shoulders sag. "Just what I needed."

He grabbed his cup and took a quick sip. "I thought I was what you needed?" He frowned slightly.

I took a long drink from my mug. "I need this to keep up with you," I joked.

He laughed, deep in his chest. "I better put on another pot then." His eyes drifted down my body and back up to my eyes.

"We can't. We have to go see my aunt today." I took another long sip.

He sighed and gulped down the rest of his cup. "I guess we better get it over with then." He clenched his jaw, looking down at his mug.

"It's not life or death, William. Worst thing that is going to happen is she will call me a whore and things will be exactly as they have

37

always been." I rolled my eyes at the thought and took another drink.

His eyes stayed on me, lost in thought for a moment. "Fine." He sat his cup down hard on the counter and brushed passed me, heading towards his bedroom.

William emerged a few moments later, pulling a dark grey t-shirt over his head, covering up his chiseled abs. His eyes followed mine and he glanced down at his stomach.

"You sure you don't want to have a little fun first?" His smile was lopsided and it was a very tempting offer. I smiled back but shook my head no.

"Come on. Let's just get this over with." I sat my cup down on the island and grabbed my purse. I held my hand out for his. He stepped to my side and pulled me against him before lacing his fingers in mine. His lips pushed hard against mine and I immediately relaxed into him, letting my lips part slightly. His tongue slid along my upper lip, coaxing it my mouth open further. He deepened the kiss and I breathed a small moan into his mouth. I felt him grow hard against my hip. My body reflexively moved against him.

His lips left mine and I suddenly felt alone. I opened my eyes and he was staring down at me, lust in his eyes.

"I need you." His voice was low, and I could tell he was struggling not to take me right where we stood. I put my free hand on his chest to hold him back slightly.

"I promise when we get back you can take me any way and anywhere you like." I smiled, my teeth digging into my bottom lip. His eyebrow shot up as he thought that over for a minute. His hand slid from behind my back and he used his thumb to free my lip from my teeth. He let his thumb slide over it for a moment.

"Let's go." He tugged on my hand pulled me quickly through the front door. I giggled as he practically dragged me down the steps.

Chapter Five

As we pulled up outside of my aunt's house, my heart began to pound out of my chest. What if this was a bad idea? I swallowed hard and William grabbed my hand, giving it a gentle squeeze. His eyes were on me, pinning me in my seat.

"Having second thoughts?" he asked, using his free hand to push the hair from my forehead.

I looked down and shook my head. I needed to do this. It was now or never. I opened my door and paused to turn back to William. He looked just as nervous as I was.

"Just give me a minute okay?" He nodded, and I leaned in to give him a quick peck on the lips before reluctantly releasing his hand and slipping out of the car.

I walked towards the house, glancing back at William. He looked deep in thought as he stared back at me. I took another calming breath and shook off my nerves. This was a huge step for us.

I glanced up, noticing my aunt's car was not in the driveway.

"You can do this," I muttered to myself as I reached for the door handle. It was unlocked and I walked inside, laying my purse on the kitchen table.

"Judy?" I yelled back through the hall as I opened the fridge and grabbed a bottle of water. I was suddenly parched as my nerves got the better of me. I took a long sip and listened. The house was quiet. "Judy? You here?" I walked back through the hall and knocked on her bedroom door. No response.

I heard the sound of a door opening on the other side of the house. I made my way back down the hall to the kitchen area where William stood.

"I was just about to call you. She's not here." My shoulders slumped as relief washed over me. He looked down and stepped forward. His arms wrapped around me, resting firmly on my ass as he pulled me against him.

"Let's go back to my place. A promise is a promise." He grinned as he lowered his lips to mine. Before our mouths could meet, we were interrupted by the faint sound of music playing.

"What's that?" I asked as I pulled out of his arms and began searching. William followed suit and the sound grew louder as we made our way down the narrow hall.

"Oh my God" I clasped my hand over my mouth, finally placing the song. "That's my aunt's ring tone! She's home!" I whispered in a panic.

"But her car wasn't in the driveway." William searched my eyes for answers but I didn't have any. I wrapped my hand around her doorknob and took a deep breath as I slowly pushed it open. The eerie creaking sound it made was straight out of a horror film.

It took a moment for my eyes to adjust to the dimness of her room. My aunt's naked lifeless body lay across her bed, legs splayed open for the world to see. Her skin was grey and her eyes stared off into the distance. Her lips parted slightly. I clasp my hands over my mouth as I struggled to register what I was seeing. Her face was bloated and her last expression was a mixture of sheer pleasure and absolute terror. My gut wrenched and I clutched at my abdomen.

"Judy!" I screamed as William grabbed my waist and pulled my back into the hallway. I struggled against him, but his grip tightened.

He stroked my hair as I completely lost control, sobbing into his chest.

"Shh..." he whispered, but I could feel his heart was beating out of his chest.

"I need to call someone!" I began to ramble. He nodded his head and kissed me hard on my forehead.

"It's going to be okay, Emma. I'm going to take care of you." He wiped the tears from my cheeks and for just a moment, I was lost in his touch.

"I'll be here the whole time." He kissed me again, letting his lips linger on my damp skin before pulling me back down the hall. He stopped in the kitchen to grab my phone.

I waited a moment before stepping out onto the driveway, William at my side. The sun was already beating down and the blacktop was burning hot under my sandals. I unlocked my phone and dialed 9-1-1.

"9-1-1, what is your emergency?" A female voice answered on the other end of the line.

"My aunt... My aunt is..." I began to sob. William took the phone from my hands and explained what we had found. I sank to my knees. When the phone call ended, William wrapped his arms around me, pulling me to my feet and into his chest.

"This can't be happening," I sobbed, gripping his shirt as if it was holding me to the earth. I didn't want to think about what all this would be like if I didn't have him.   Although it had taken that incident when I cut my hand to realize my aunt loved me, we hadn't really had a chance to get close. Still; I couldn't think about going on without her. She was the last link to my mother.

Everything was a blur. When help finally arrived, they brought everyone in the county with them. Three police cars, an ambulance, and several unmarked cars crowded my short driveway. One of the officers had been here when my aunt thought I had tried to commit suicide. I clung to William's side like I couldn't breathe without him. I wasn't sure I could.

"I need to take your statements." The officer was holding a notebook and pen in hand.

"I just came home. I didn't think she was here. I found her..." It was impossible to form a coherent sentence.

"Can you verify your whereabouts in the past twenty-four hours?" The officer's eyes flicked between William and me.

"She was with me." William squeezed me tightly against him. It was an unbelievable weight lifted off my shoulders not to have to lie to the police about us. I knew William didn't have a problem exposing our secret, but I was still worried he would one day regret it.

"Is there anyone else who can verify that?" The officer arched his eyebrow at William and squared his shoulders. William's eyes shot down to mine and back to the officer.

"We were alone." He gave the officer a small smile and something registered across the policeman's face.

The questions continued. When I couldn't find the words or emotions had taken over, William spoke with the officers. He was so composed and in control. I envied him for that. I could do no more than simply sob.

As they brought my aunt outside on a stretcher, covered by a thin white sheet, I struggled to keep my composure. Memories of my parent's death flashed in my head and it was all I could do to stay on my feet. William held me tight and turned me away from her body. The officer's eyes softened and reassured me they would find whoever had done this.

"Do you have somewhere you can go for a few days?" he asked. "This is a crime scene, and you won't be allowed back inside until we're done here."

I nodded my head and glanced to William. He squeezed me tighter into his side. This was the last place I wanted to be, especially if there was a killer still on the loose. The officer patted me on the shoulder, his eyes filled with pity. I couldn't escape that look. The whole ordeal lasted for hours. William and I had to go to the police station and give statements. I don't know what I would have done if William hadn't been with me. My mind was swimming in sorrow.

"You call me if you remember anything else that may be important," a detective said as he slid me his card. "And please stay in Florida until we have this all wrapped up. An officer will help you gather some things when you go back to the house."

When we got back to the house to get my things, there were still a lot of people around.

I watched as the garage door slowly raised and there was more commotion off to the side of the house. My aunt's car was inside, I hadn't even thought to look. I covered my mouth and grabbed my stomach. What if the killer had still been inside when I arrived?

Chapter Six

One of the officers escorted me to my room long enough to grab a bag of clothes.

William led me to his car and opened the passenger door for me. I got in and we rode to his place in silence. I stared out of the car window wishing he would never stop driving. I wanted to run away from my life.

As we pulled into the garage his building, I finally broke down, quietly sobbing into my hands. William got out and was quickly by my side. He slid me out of my seat and carried me upstairs as I continued to cry into his neck. He took me straight into his bedroom, keeping the light off. He lowered me gently onto the bed as he crawled behind me and pulled me tight against his body. I finally felt safe and I let my sobs take over. He stroked my arm soothingly as I lost all control.

After what seemed like an eternity, I was able to stop the loud sobs. Tears silently slid down my face as we lay in each other's arms.

"I can help distance the pain," he whispered in my ear. I turned my head to look at him over my shoulder. He squeezed me tightly. "Let me take it all away for you."

I nodded slightly and his hand slid over my stomach as I rolled to my back. His body hovered over mine as he began to undress me slowly. He pulled my shirt over my head, followed by his own. He made quick work of our pants and soon we lay naked as he lowered himself onto me.

"I love you so much, Emma." His mouth found mine and his kisses were slow and sweet. His body rocked against me gently and I let my legs fall to the sides. He was taking his time.

My hands dug into his back. I wanted him hard and full of passion, but he refused. He took his time trailing kisses along my jaw and down the nape of my neck. I sighed as his lips traced my collarbone.

"Please…" I panted as his mouth found my nipple and he flicked it with his tongue. I could feel him grow harder as he pressed against my leg. My fingers knotted onto his hair.

"Please, William. I need you." I wasn't above begging him. I wanted to forget everything. His mouth continued to descend as he licked and kissed his way to my belly button. His tongue dipped inside, and I squirmed against him. His lips moved over one of my hipbones and I bit my lip to keep from crying out. I raised my hips towards him, desperate for him to touch me. His tongue slid down my inner thigh and kissed its way back up. I pulled lightly on his hair. His breath blew over my most sensitive areas as he gave my other thigh equal treatment. All I could think about was William's mouth. I rested my head back as he drifted closer to my center with light feathery kisses down the apex of my thighs.

"Ahh… please," I begged, pushing down. His arms wrapped around my legs, holding me firmly in place. His tongue slipped over me and my body quivered. "Yes," I panted as he used his fingers to spread me open further. His lips slid along my wetness as he pushed his tongue inside. His fingers knew all the right buttons to push as he made love to me with his mouth. I gripped his hair tighter as I gave into the pleasure. His tongue continued to explore as he pushed one of his fingers inside of me. I began to rotate my hips against him as he continued to lick and nip. He added another finger. My body bucked against him as I began my release.

"Let go," he moaned. I completely fell to pieces as my body tightened around his fingers. He licked and kissed until my body relaxed. I released his hair from my grip and he slid up my body.

"Thank you," I whispered, wrapping my arms around him.

"We're just getting started." He slipped himself inside of me and began rocking his hips.

Chapter Seven

After I had had all the forgetting my body could handle from William, he forced me to get dressed and leave the bedroom. I wanted to curl into a ball, but he refused to let me mope. He sat me on the couch and handed me the remote to find something to watch while he cooked us something to eat for dinner. I hadn't realized how hungry I was until I smelled the food cooking. I hadn't had anything all day besides coffee.

I flipped through the channels, pausing on a news broadcast. It took me a moment to realize why it looked so familiar. The reporter stood in front of my aunt's home and told of a horrific murder. A picture of my aunt flashed across the screen and I put my hand over my mouth from the shock.

William was quickly by my side. He pulled the remote from my hand a flicked through a couple channels before dropping it and pulling me into him.

"Shh... It's okay." His hand stroked my hair.

"I can't do this," I whispered into his shoulder. His body tensed but quickly relaxed.

"I'll help you through this," he promised.

I squeezed him and nodded as one of my tears fell onto his shirt.

"Nothing can hurt you anymore. I won't let it." There was a steel determination in his voice as his hand drifted to my back as he rubbed it.

"Thank you." I kissed his neck and he pulled back from me. He wiped my tears with the back of his hand. I grabbed it with my hand and held it there, closing my eyes.

"Let's get you something to eat." He stood from the couch and held onto my hand, pulling me to my feet. He led me to the bar in the kitchen and I sat on a stool as he walked around and grabbed two plates. He sat one down in front of me and my stomach immediately growled. He had made subs, complete with a handful of chips on the side.

"Thank you," I said as I popped a barbeque chip in my mouth.

"It's not my best cooking, but I figured you had to be hungry." He ran a hand through his hair and took a seat next to me.

"No, I mean for everything. For being there for me." I smiled at him. His fingers tipped my chin up to look him in the eyes.

"I'm not going anywhere, Emma. You couldn't get rid of me if you tried." He laughed and my smile grew.

"Why would I ever want to get rid of you?"

He shook his head and turned back to his plate.

"Eat. You need your energy." With that, we both ate in silence. I tried my best not to think of the latest loss in my life. Instead, I counted my blessing. William was a blessing. It made my heart ache that he didn't think so. He seemed always to be waiting for the moment that I told him I didn't want him anymore. I made a mental note to kick Abby's ass if I ever saw her again for all the pain she had caused him. I knew it wasn't entirely her fault. His parent's had been equally responsible for how damaged he had become.

I glanced over at him as he finished his sandwich. I had barely taken a few bites of mine.

I felt his eyes on me and glanced over at him.

"You have barely touched your food." He gestured towards my plate.

"I'm not really that hungry." I shrugged and sat my sandwich down.

"Eat," he said sternly.

"I'm really not that…"

He cut me off, his eyes hard and cold. "I'm not asking." With that, he got up and took his plate to the sink. I picked up my sandwich and took another bite.

I watched him wash the dishes as I shoveled the food into my mouth. His muscles pulled under shirt as he washed and dried the dishes, and then again, when he reached to place them in the cabinets. God he was perfect.

He moved to the fridge and grabbed a soda, sitting it down in front of me. I popped the last bite into my mouth and nodded to thank him.

"Good girl." His fingertips traced along my jaw as he grinned.

My face flushed and his words sent electricity throughout my body. How did he do that? He made me forget anything bad in my life. My world revolved around him now. I swallowed and cracked open my soda as he turned back to the fridge and grabbed a bottle of amber liquid. He grabbed a few glasses from under the island and sat them in front of us.

"I don't know about you, but it has been a long day and I could use a drink." He grinned as he poured some of the alcohol into the glasses.

"Thanks." I smiled and picked up the glass, smelling it. "Ohh..." I said pulling the glass away from my face. He laughed. It resonated from deep in his chest.

"Don't ever hesitate. You have to just go for it or you will talk yourself out of it." He pushed my hand back towards me. I took a deep breath and drank it down. It burned its way down my throat and I slammed down the empty glass and grabbed my soda, chugging a long sip. He laughed again and grabbed the bottle to pour another drink. He shook his head, highly amused.

"Again. This time, no chaser." He sat the glass in front of me again, and I eyed it cautiously. "Drink it," he said slowly, enunciating each word.

I grabbed the glass and dumped the fiery liquid down my throat. I coughed slightly and brought my hand up to my lips.

He smiled and drank back his glass down effortlessly. He sat it down with a solid thud. "Good girl."

I beamed with pride at the way he praised me.

"More?" He held up the bottle.

I nodded and bit my lip as I waited for the next drink. My body was already warning and I felt like I could finally relax.

We drank again, this time I didn't cough. Instead, I yelled. "Woo!" I sat my glass back on the counter and slid it towards him. He licked his lips and glanced back at my face.

"I think that is enough for now."

I pouted and he reached over the counter, rubbing my bottom lip with the pad of his thumb. "Let's go have some fun." He tilted his head towards the elevator and raised an eyebrow. I blushed and looked down at my glass as he made his way around the counter and took my hand.

Chapter Eight

The night was a blur of pleasure and pain. William guided me to a high bench. He made me strip off all of my clothes except for my panties. I lay my body down over the cold vinyl and waited for him to secure my hands above my head. When he finished he moved to my legs, spreading them as wide as they would go. He didn't tie them down. Instead, he whispered a warning into my ear.

"If you move your legs, I will punish you." My body went rigid. He added, "You will fucking love it."

I sighed. His words did amazing things to me. I couldn't wait to feel him touch me. I craved it. I needed it. He pulled back and I heard him doing something behind me. The anticipation was killing me.

"Do you remember the safe word?" He asked as his fingertips trailed light up the back of my thigh.

"Oh... god..."

Something came down fast and hard against my backside. I squealed with pain.

"Wrong." His hand came down again. The stinging sensation was soon replaced with the soft tingle of his fingertips. He ran his hand over my aching backside and ghosted over my wetness.

"Flower," I panted. As the words left my mouth his finger dipped inside of me. "Ahh... yes... flower."

His fingers stopped and he pulled out of me, leaving me empty and aching for more. He leaned over, his breath tickling my ear.

"Are you using your safe word?" His eyebrows were pulled together.

"What? No… no…" I turned my head to look at him. He smiled and swatted my bottom.

"Stay still." He repositioned himself behind me.

I giggled, the alcohol definitely making me feel more adventurous.

His hand slid over me and it was moist. A warming sensation followed the trail left by his fingertips. He slid over my folds and I pressed my lips together, trying not to moan.

He chuckled softly. "You can moan. I want to hear you enjoying this." His fingers slid down over me again, this time pulling back further until he reached my lower back. I stiffened as his fingers brushed over my ass.

"Just enjoy it, Emma," he encouraged as his other hand slid over my bottom. He reached between my thighs. I relaxed again as rubbed small circles on my nub.

"Oh… god!"

His other hand dipped two fingers inside of me and pulled back to rub over me again. I didn't flinch this time as he slipped over my backside. His other hand was too distracting to care.

"Good girl," he praised. I smiled to myself as he repeated the process over and over. His fingers trailed up my ass, spreading the warm liquid. This time he pushed against my smaller hole with his finger. I gasped and tugged against my wrist restraints.

"Shh…" I felt something else now at my entrance. His hardness pushed into my folds and I cried out as his finger went deeper in my ass. His hips moved against me quickly.

It was an odd sensation, being filled so completely. It was also very terrifying.

"William," I panted as he continued to grind into me.

"Emma, I want you. Every part of you. I can't help myself." His words melted away any concern I had. I ground back against him. He let out a primal groan.

"Let me take you. Please let me take you. I can't wait any longer." He slipped out of me. I immediately missed our connection. He positioned himself at my backside, gripping onto my hip painfully tight. "Relax." His hand slipped off my hip and around me, sliding against my throbbing core.

"Ahh… yes!" He pushed against my ass, slipping inside slightly. "Ahh…" I cried out in a mix of pleasure and pain. His fingers worked faster.

"Do you want me to stop?" His breathing was heavy. My body began to shake with impending release.

"No." My words came out in a deep moan. He pushed against me slipping further inside.

Painfully slow, he pushed himself into me. The stretching and burning sensation was almost too much. When I felt his hips finally lay against me, I breathed out hard.

"This is mine, Emma. Every part of you is mine." He slowly pulled back. The feeling was overwhelming. "Tell me, Emma. I need to hear you say it."

I struggled to catch my breath.

"Every part of me is yours."

His pace quickened slightly as he continued the small circles with his fingers. I felt my body responding to his desire and I was on the verge of coming.

"Mine," he panted as he pumped harder into me.

"Yes... I belong to you... William." I cried out as it all became too much. My words triggered his release and he stilled behind me as we both came together.

"Jesus Christ," he growled as he slowly removed himself.

He undid my wrists and I stumbled as I tried to stand. My entire body ached and I knew once the alcohol wore off it would be much worse.

William gathered our clothing and wrapped his arm around my waist as he guided me to the elevator doors. I leaned against his body as we rode down to his main living area.

He walked me to the bedroom and I sat down at the foot of the bed as he turned and quickly left the room. My heart stopped beating for a second as I thought of him pushing me away again as he used to. I moved and crawled under the covers, curling up on my side.

William retuned with a glass of water and a bottle of aspirin. He stopped short of the bed and his expression changed.

"What's wrong? Did I hurt you?"

I realized that his new look was of panic.

"No... no... it's nothing. I'm fine."

He took a hesitant step closer. "Are you sure?" he asked.

I pushed myself up into a sitting position. "It's nothing a little medicine and your touch can't cure." I smiled and he returned the gesture.

"Here. I thought you may be a little sore." He handed me the glass of water and opened the pill bottle, dumping two into the palm of his hand. I took the pills and popped them into my mouth. I took a long sip of water, then handed him the glass.

"Thank you."

He smiled again and climbed into the bed, wrapping his arms around me and pulling me against him. I listened for his breathing to steady and deepen. When he finally drifted off, I allowed myself to relax and get some sleep.

Chapter Nine

My head throbbed and I groaned at the light that filled the room.

"You okay?" Williams hand stroked the side of my face, looking like he had broken his favorite toy. I smiled slightly and struggled to open my eyes.

"I've been better." I looked over at him. He was frowning. "It was worth it, though."

He smiled and wrapped his hand in my hair, pulling my mouth to his.

"Mmmm..." I moaned as I felt him grow even happier against my thigh. It was surprising how my body always responded to William. He did something to me that I never thought was possible. He kissed me quickly on the forehead and pulled back from me.

"Where are you going?" I huffed and propped myself up on my elbow. He turned around to shoot me a smile and grabbed the bottle of aspirin off the dresser. He handed me two and the water from last night. I took them gratefully as my eyes danced over his hard naked body. God, he was perfect.

"Come on." He inclined his head towards the door. I furrowed my brow as I handed him back the glass of water.

"Where are we going?" I asked as I slipped out from under the covers and planted my feet on the ground. He grabbed my hand and pulled to a standing position. His manhood brushing against my thigh. The look in his eyes turned to desire.

"Let's go get cleaned up before we get ourselves dirty again." He grinned wickedly and pulled me behind him to the bathroom.

I watched him as he adjusted the water until he got it at just the right temperature. He turned back to me and ran his fingers over my cheek. My face heated at his intense gaze.

"You are so beautiful."

My knees went weak with his words. I waited for him to laugh, or crack a smile but he remained serious. I looked down at my feet but his fingers grabbed my chin, tilting it toward him.

"You really are."

I tucked my hair behind my ear, my eyes dancing over his perfectly chiseled face. His hand began to stroke my hair.

"You have no idea, do you?" He leaned in and pressed his lips against my forehead. "My beautiful broken girl." He sighed and led me into the tub.

I dipped my toe into the water to check the temperature.

"Good?" he asked, leaning in to see my face.

"Perfect." I smiled over at him as I lowered myself into the tub. He reached over and shut off the water before slipping in behind me.

I relaxed my arms on his knees as he grabbed some liquid soap and poured it into the palm of his hand. His hand slid over my breast as he began to wash me.

His fingers hesitated for a moment.

"What?" I asked.

His hands slowly started to move again. "We need to start thinking about funeral arrangements." His voice was low. I swallowed hard and nodded my head. I didn't want to think about any of that, but there was no one else.

He didn't say anything else. His hands roamed my body making sure every part of me was clean. He didn't turn it into anything sexual and I was glad. My mind was somewhere else.

After he was finished lathering me up, I turned around and returned the favor. As my hands moved down his body, he grabbed my wrist and stared at me for a moment before letting me continue on to the hard shaft between his legs. His head fell back for a moment, and he swallowed hard, trying, I knew, not to let his hormones take over.

"That is enough of that." He smiled and climbed out of the tub.

I realized that the water had long since lost its warmth. I shivered as I stood, and William wrapped an oversized white towel around my shoulders. His own towel hung low on his hips.

"Thank you." I shot him a half smile as I followed him out of the bathroom.

He nodded and ran his hand through his wet hair, sending water droplets sprinkling over me.

"I mean it. For everything."

He stopped and spun around, wrapping his muscular arms around my waist, and lifted me to my toes to kiss him.

"I love you, Emma. There is nothing I wouldn't do for you."

I let my fingers slip into his hair and tugged it gently as I kissed him. He eased me back down and walked towards the kitchen.

He handed me my phone and urged me to call the police department to see when the body could be released. I grabbed the detective's card from my purse for the number, and bit my nails as I waited for an answer.

William worked his way around the kitchen, throwing together something for us to eat.

Most of what the detective said went in one ear and out the other. I was so overcome with emotion, it was hard to focus. I hung up the phone and let my head fall in my hands.

"What did they say?" William asked as he placed a bowl of hot tomato soup and a grilled cheese sandwich in front of me. My stomach growled.

"Thanks." I picked up my spoon and took a small bite.

"What did they say?" he asked again.

"They said her death was... insulin overdose." I tore off a piece of my sandwich and dipped it into the bowl of creamy red liquid.

"That's a good thing, right? You don't have to worry about anyone coming back to hurt you." William picked up his sandwich and began to eat.

"I guess. I never realized being diabetic was that serious. I just don't believe she is gone." I took another bite as I watched him ravish his food. Nothing kept William from missing a meal.

"They said I can make the arrangements."

He didn't respond, just nodded his head as he continued to eat.

After William saw to it that I ate my entire meal, he began to call around and helped me make arrangements for Judy's funeral.

Chapter Ten

We drove to Jacoby's Funeral home just a few blocks from William's place. It was a small brick building just off the main strip in town. William squeezed my hand and brought it to his lips.

"I'll be there with you. You don't have to worry about anything." He waited for me to nod a response before letting my hand fall from his. He exited the Beamer and made his way to my side. He pulled the door open and held his hand out for me to take.

I didn't let his hand go until every last decision had been made. William made most of the arrangements, leaving only the casket and location of burial to me.

By the time we left, my head was spinning. My aunt would be buried at Mt. Rose Cemetery in two days. I was happy that this would finally be over soon. I didn't know how much more I could take.

My aunt and I didn't get along that well, but I still loved her and she was the only family I had left. I tried not to think of the humiliation she would feel if word got out that she had died in the middle of some sex act, but she must have, since she was naked. She brought home lots of men, sure, but I still didn't believe it.

"Let's get you back home." William slid his arm around my waist as we made our way back to his car.

I cranked the radio in William's car until it drowned out my thoughts. I didn't want to think anymore. I wanted these next two days to fly by so I could put this chapter behind me.

William watched me as I stared ahead. As the first song finished he turned down the volume slightly.

"You want to talk… about anything?"

There were a million things I wanted to say to him. I wanted to confess my anger for not taking the time to get to know my aunt better. I wanted to tell him about my parents. Words failed me. I shook my head and reach for the stereo to crank it back up to deafening levels. He gripped the steering wheel and didn't say anything else.

We reached his home in record time. I didn't wait for him to open my door. I felt like I was suffocating. I needed to get upstairs as quickly as possible. William took the stairs two at a time to catch me as I made it to his door. I leaned my head against the cold hard surface, fighting back my tears.

What would I do if he decided that I was too much trouble? That I wasn't worth it?

His arms wrapped around my body and he pulled me into his chest. I felt safe when I was in his arms. I only felt safe when I was there.

He reached behind me and unlocked the door. His arm dipped under my knees and he lifted me into his arms and carried me inside. He placed me gently on the couch and brushed the hair from my face.

"What is it?" His voice was warm and caring.

"I'm going to lose you too, aren't I?" I held my breath as I waited for him to tell me I was right. That my whole world was going to implode.

He pressed his forehead against mine as he continued to stroke my hair.

"Never, Emma. You are my everything. I could never leave you. You would be impossible to forget. Why would you even think that?"

I nodded as my hand twisted in his hair.

"I love you," he said gently.

"I love you, too. So much."

"Wait here." William kissed me lightly on the forehead and left the room. I waited, wondering what he was doing.

A moment later, he returned with a square cardboard box in his hands.

"What is that?" I laughed, cocking my head to the side.

"This, my dear, is a distraction." He sat down in the middle of the floor and motioned for me to join him.

"Yatzee? Really?" I laughed as I sat down across from him and folded my legs under myself.

"What? You expected Parcheesi?"

I made face at him as he opened the box and we each rolled to see who went first.

That game turned into ten and before I knew it, I was yawning and stretching across the floor like a cat.

"Quitting already?"

I smiled and propped myself up on my elbow.

"Thank you... for everything." He had no idea just how much it meant to me. I needed the distraction.

He winked and pushed himself off the floor, holding out his hand for me. I wrapped my fingers in his and let him pull me to my feet and against his chest.

"One more day to go," he said as he kissed the top of my head.

I knew as long as I had William, everything was going to be okay.

Chapter Eleven

"Oh...mmmm..." I pushed back against the fingers that slid over my mound. I opened my eyes to see William's face watching me as his fingers traced the delicate curves of my body. "That is the best wakeup call I have ever received."

"It's not over yet." He smiled as he ducked his head to my chest, pinching my nipple between his teeth. I arched my back, desperate for more contact. His tongue gently pushed back against me.

"Ahh..." His fingers, wet with my excitement, slipped lower. He traced my entrance before slipping one finger inside of my folds. His tongue swirled small circled over my breast as pleasure began to build between my thighs. I reached for him, slipping my hand behind his neck. His free hand grabbed my wrist tightly.

He pulled it to his mouth and peppered light kisses over it before pushing it down on the pillow above my head.

I squirmed against him, trying to pull my hand free. His lips trailed along my ear.

"I like it when you fight."

A moan escaped my lips and I brought my hips up to grind against his hand. His palm rubbed against me as he slipped another finger inside. I used my free hand to push against his chest. He grinned wickedly as he pressed his body against mine.

"Bad girl." He kissed me hard, pulling back to tug my bottom lip between his teeth. I pushed against him, bucking my hips. His fingers left my body and he grabbed my other hand, securing it above my head with the other. I was helpless beneath him and loving every minute of it, except for the aching emptiness

Teresa Mummert

between my thighs. He smiled again as if reading my thoughts.

"I want to hear you beg for it."

My stubbornness kicked in, and I clamped my mouth shut, refusing to give in. His hips pushed into mine as he throbbed against my entrance.

"Ohh…" My mouth fell back open.

"Do you want me?" His hips moved again, his hand slipping between my folds.

"Yes," I panted. I lifted my head to kiss him but he pulled his face back, smiling.

"Tell me you want me." He pulled back slightly and I tugged my arms, trying desperately to free my hands from his grip. I needed to touch him.

"I want you, William."

With one hard thrust, he buried himself deep inside of me. I gasped and cried out. His mouth quickly covered mine, absorbing my moans as he took me rough and without caution. My core burned with pleasure as he filled and stretched me. His fingers curled and dug into my flesh of my wrists as his release neared.

I forgot everything painful in my life when I was with him. He stole my sadness away with his touch. I couldn't get enough. It didn't matter if he was gentle or rough.

I rocked my hips as our bodies pounded together, fitting so perfectly. We were made for each other. He broke our kiss to look me in the eye.

"Tell me you belong to me."

"I'm yours, William," I moaned as he pushed violently against me as he came, sending me over the edge of pleasure with him. My legs went limp as he collapsed his body on top of mine.

After catching our breath, we took a long soothing soak in the tub. We talked of random events in our lives to keep the mood light. He never let me think of my aunt's death.

"Tell me about your first kiss?" I asked as William swirled circles of soap on my knee.

"Junior High. She slapped me." He laughed as he recalled the memory.

"Quite the lady killer." I laughed and William's hand stilled.

"Got you, didn't I?" he whispered in my ear.

"I didn't mean to offend-"

"You didn't." He slowly started to rub the soap over my leg again.

"What about pets?" I asked.

"I got a golden retriever for Christmas when I was ten. Her name was Lacey. She was a great dog." I could hear the smile in his voice. "What about you?"

"My mother was highly allergic to pet dander. I was never allowed to have a dog." I sighed.

His hands slid up to my shoulders and he began to rub the tension from them. "We can get a dog one day."

The idea made me smile from ear to ear.

"I'm beginning to prune." I laughed and held up my fingers. William slipped from behind me and grabbed a towel for each of us.

I dried off and threw on an old pair of jeans and a tank top. William dressed in a navy blue vintage t-shirt and dark blue jeans.

I cooked a nice brunch for the both of us. William settled in at the island, clearly not happy about not being in control in his own kitchen.

"I need to get these smoke detectors upgraded if you are going to take over cooking in my kitchen," he groused.

I shot him a glare over my shoulder as I prepared our omelets.

"Careful," he warned, raising his eyebrow at me.

My cheeks flushed pink and I turned back to the food on the stove. "So... what are our plans for today?"

"I was thinking we could rent a movie, cuddle on the couch." He got up from his seat and began to prepare a pot of coffee. We danced around each other as we got our breakfast together. It was nice.

"A movie sounds great."

I dished out our breakfast and took my usual seat at the island. William sat the coffee cups on the table and sat next to me.

"This is nice, having you here all the time." He took a bite from his food.

It was nice. It felt natural. We worked well together. I wanted to be able to stay with him forever, but I knew it was a bad idea. William's father hated me, and he could disinherit him or cut off his money. I was still worried about his job, too. No one would offer a teaching position to a professor that was sleeping with a previous student, I was sure—despite what he said about it not mattering since I'd graduated. We already have taken too many risks.

I took a bite of my omelet and made a face. It was awful. William never complained; bless his heart. I took a few more bites. If he could suffer through my cooking, so could I.

When we finished our meal, it was already well after noon. I was thankful William was keeping me busy enough not to worry about all of the things going on outside of our relationship.

After we cleared the dishes and finished off our pot of coffee, we drove down to the local movie store.

I made a beeline for the romantic comedies. William just raised an eyebrow and wandered around the other rows.

"What about this one?" I asked, holding up the latest blockbuster about a female bounty hunter.

He frowned and held up a gory slasher film. I made a face at him but couldn't stop myself from laughing.

"Fine, if you throw in some popcorn it's a deal," I said, caving in.

He rounded the end of the row and looped his arm around my waist. "Good girl." He smiled and my insides melted.

We went back to William's place. I prepared the popcorn as he popped in the disc and grabbed the pillows from the other couch. I sat down on the couch and William disappeared into his room. He returned a moment later with the heavy comforter from his bed and laid it out over the sofa for us to cuddle under. I leaned against him and he placed his arm around me as the movie began.

We only got about ten minutes into the film until his free hand slid over my thigh and he was breathing heavily into my neck.

"I'm actually enjoying this," I laughed and pointed to the screen just as the killer was chasing a girl up a flight of stairs. She tripped and he grabbed her by her ankle, dragging her back down to him. I winced and snuggled deeper into William's side. He chuckled, his breath tickling my neck.

"William," I giggled. "Arggh!" The killer stabbed his poor victim in the chest.

His laughter was deep in his chest now, obviously amused by me. His hand slid further up my leg.

"Don't you want to see him get caught?" I asked, shoving a handful of popcorn in my mouth.

"How do you know he won't get away with it?" William grabbed a handful and shoved it in his mouth.

"They never get away with it. Come on. They always leave some sort of clues behind. It's like they want to get caught." I rolled my eyes and watched the screen intently.

"You think that guy wants to get caught?" He pointed at the killer who was still in his victim's home, waiting for her guests to arrive.

"Subconsciously, yes."

William looked at me as if I was crazy.

"Stupid does not mean he wants to get caught. It just means he's not smart enough to do it right."

"Whatever." I threw a piece of popcorn at him and sighed.

"Bad girl." He tackled me, pinning me underneath him on the couch, which sent popcorn spilling everywhere. The moment his hips pressed against mine, the mood shifted from playful to something else.

"We are gonna miss the movie."

"Fuck the movie." His tongue pushed into my mouth. He lowered me back until he was resting fully on top of me. "I want to make you scream like you did a minute ago."

He pulled my shirt over my head and tossed it across the room as he sat up long enough to pull his over his head. The lights from the television danced off his bare chest. He fell back on top of me, his hand finding my right breast and gently caressing it as he deepened our kiss. His fingers pinched my nipple and pulled it.

"Fuck the movie," I breathed, and he smiled as he began to unbutton my jeans and slide them down my legs. He backed his way off the couch as he removed them fully, along with my panties.

He stood looking down at me as he slowly undid his belt and shoved down his pants and boxers.

"Stand up," he commanded. I slowly pushed myself off the couch to stand in front of him. He grabbed my hips and spun me around.

"Put your knees on the couch and hold on to the back."

As I did, he grabbed my hips and pulled me back to him. He nudged my legs apart. "Wider."

He positioned himself at my entrance from behind. I glanced over my shoulder at him, chewing on my lip.

"Don't worry. I'm not going to hurt you." He kissed my cheek and gently slid inside my throbbing folds from behind.

"God, you're so fucking wet for me." His breath on my ear made me melt. His fingers gripped tighter on my hips as he slowly picked up his pace. I pushed my backside into him as I held on tight to the back of the couch. One of his hands slid up my spine and wrapped in my hair. He made a fist and pulled my head back as his bucked harder. He leaned over me.

"You like it when I'm rough with you?" His lips hovered next to mine. I tried to turn to him, to kiss him, but he held my hair firm in his grip.

"Yes," I moaned. The hand on his hip slipped in front of me, rubbing small circles over my mound. "Oh…"

My walls began to tighten around him and his hand stopped moving. I was so close. His strokes became longer and slower, waiting for my body to relax. When it did, his pace resumed and his fingers found that magic spot again.

I pushed my ass back against him with each thrust.

"Come for me, Emma," he whispered and my body unraveled around him. I cried out as I felt him let go and come inside of me. I collapsed over the back of the couch, his sweat slicked chest falling onto my back.

"I love you," he said as he pushed the hair off my forehead. He pulled out of me and sat back onto the couch. "Come on, you're going to the miss the part where he gets caught." He smirked and slapped me hard on the ass.

I yelped and spun around to sit next to him. I grabbed a few pieces of popcorn that had fallen on the blanket and popped them in my mouth as I settled into his side.

We watched the rest of the movie and then settled on some TV before falling asleep in each other's arms on the couch. I loved it when he held me tight against him. I felt safe.

Chapter Twelve

The funeral was held in the small cemetery on the edge of town. Nothing stood out about the place. The stones were all small and plain. A few big trees dotted the edge of the property. The last time I had been to a funeral was for my parents. The thought made me cringe. I had no one left now. No one but William.

I glanced over in his direction. His face was hard. His jaw muscles flexed below his skin as he stared off in the distance. I swallowed back the lump in my throat. He reached over and placed his hand on my knee, giving it a firm squeeze. His eyes never glanced in my direction. I wanted him to wrap his arms around me and to tell me everything was going to be okay, but he was lost in his own thoughts. I placed my hand on top of his and rubbed the back of it gently.

He looked down at them and then finally let his eyes meet mine. "I'm sorry."

I nodded, unable to form any words. I blew out the breath I hadn't realized I'd been holding. My aunt and I had never really gotten along, but I never realized just how much I loved her.

Tears began to trickle down my cheeks. William gave one last gentle squeeze and exited the car. He made his way to my side and opened my door, holding out his hand for me. I took it and he pulled me into his arms, holding me while I quietly broke down in his arms.

The sky was overcast, and the world had a dingy hue. It seemed fitting on a day that you buried someone. I smoothed out my skirt and took a long deep breath before nodding to William that I was ready.

My heels sank into the dampened grass and I silently cursed myself for not wearing sensible shoes. I wanted to break down and cry over my stupid choice of footwear. I glanced up at the small crowd of people ahead.

"Do you know them?" William asked, leaning into me so no one would hear our conversation. I narrowed my eyes and looked ahead. The only people I ever saw with my aunt were the men that came in and out of our house at all hours of the night. I shook my head no and looked to the ground as we approached.

Sad smiles and teary eyes greeted us. Several women shook my hand and offered me condolences along with looks of pity. I would never escape those looks.

I smiled weakly at the minister who returned the gesture. I wanted this to be a distant memory as soon as possible. He began speaking as the small crowd formed a semicircle around the large wooden box in front of us. William positioned himself behind me, his hand placed gently on my lower back. Several more people filed around as the man spoke sweet words about a woman he had never even met. I found that even more depressing. His words flew over my head and I wasn't able to focus on anything he said.

As the service ended, I began the awkward phase of greeting and thanking everyone who had taken the time to say goodbye to my aunt. It was like having an out of body experience. My brain wasn't registering anything that was said.

The only thing that snapped me out of my daze was William's hand leaving my back. I glanced over my shoulder and watched him make his way through the small crowd, following a woman in a sleek black dress. Panic washed over me as I wondered if it was someone who worked at Kippling with him.

My thoughts flashed to Angela but I quickly pushed her out of my mind.

I turned back to face the grieving woman in front of me as my stomach twisted in knots. My feet felt like they were stuck in cement. I was too scared to go to him. Would he leave me too? Leave me with nothing? I was terrified and I almost breathed a sigh of relief as the woman finished giving me her condolences. I glanced back over my shoulder, searching the cemetery for William.

I spotted him under a large elm tree. William looked angry as he leaned in closely to speak to the woman. Her fingers were tracing the button line of William's shirt and he reached up to grab her hands, angrily pushing them away. It was an oddly intimate moment. His face was close to hers and cocked to the side. Her body leaned in toward him.

My heart stopped beating. His eyes met mine and I tried unsuccessfully to erase the look of sheer horror on my face.

My feet began to move swiftly as if they had a mind of their own. My mind raced with the thought of William and another woman. I tried to shake the idea. I was upset and I wasn't thinking clearly. The fear kept me going. I needed to know who that woman was and why she was at my aunt's funeral. Nothing made sense. Hot tears stung at my eyes and the vision of them became a blur. I saw them separate, stepping unnaturally far apart for something innocent.

I didn't care. I was at a funeral. There was nothing out of place about someone grieving. As I reached them, my knees became weak and I struggled to stand on my own accord.

"Emma." William didn't sound like his normal calm and in control self. There was something else in his voice, fear maybe?

I wiped at my face to dash away the tears. The woman before me had her arms crossed over her chest. She was a stunning brunette. I looked her up and down before looking back at William, hoping she didn't mean anything to him. I never once considered that there was anyone else. I suddenly felt foolish and... jealous. All of the anger and sadness I had been trying desperately to suppress came bubbling to the surface.

"This is..." He gestured to the leggy brunette. She took a step forward, hand extended.

"Allison." She smiled and I wanted to attack. Instead, I ignored her hand and turned back to William. "I should probably go."

I gave Allison a look of disgust and watched her turn and head for her car. I folded my arms over my chest and prepared for an all-out battle.

"Who is she?" I asked, my teeth grinding together painfully hard.

"She is no one." His voice was stern and he glanced around making sure no one was listening to our conversation. The last few people had made their way to their cars.

"Fuck them." My words came out louder than I intended, but I didn't care. I had nothing left to lose. Nothing but him. My heart was breaking.

"Let me take you back to my place." He stepped forward and placed his hands on my arms, rubbing them. I pulled back from him, planting myself against the large tree.

"Did you…" I couldn't get the words to pass my lips. I searched him with my eyes. He clenched his jaw and his hands balled into fists at his sides.

"Don't do this here." His words were cold.

"I'll do whatever the fuck I want."

The look of shock on his face was priceless. He took a second to regain his composure and stepped closer to me, his body hovering over mine.

"She is nobody." His eyes locked onto mine.

I leaned closer to him. "Was she your girlfriend?" I searched his face for answers.

"It's not like that. We met at a club she... works at."

"Did you fuck her?"

He moved back slightly, but didn't respond. My entire world crashed down around me in his silence. I pushed against him to free myself from my position. He grabbed my shoulder, forcing me back against the tree. The bark bit into my back.

"Let me explain." He placed a hand on either side of me on the tree, keeping me pinned.

"It's a yes or no question." I pushed against his chest with both hands but he didn't move. I glanced around the cemetery. The few people that had attended the funeral had left. We were alone. William's heart raced under my fingertips.

"Please, fucking listen to me."

"Why was she here?" Tears continued to pour down my face. He looked down and didn't answer. "Why was she here?" I repeated bitterly.

He grabbed my wrists and pinned them to my sides, putting his body flush against mine.

"Get off of me!" I fought against him, but he was too strong. He growled as he struggled to keep me there. I was emotionally and physically exhausted. I sagged against the tree, sobbing.

"No one before you matters." He nuzzled my neck, relaxing into me.

"Don't," I choked out. I wanted to run away from what was left of my life.

"Please." His words were desperate. His lips moved over my neck, leaving a tiny trail of kisses. I flinched and pulled back from him. His breathing grew heavy and his chest pushed against mine. "Emma, don't leave me," his words barely a whisper but the desperation could be heard for miles.

I closed my eyes, trying to stop the flow of tears.

"Tell me you love me." He tried to look in my eyes but I turned my head away from him. He let go of my wrists and moved his hands to either side of my face, forcing me to look in his direction.

"I don't want to," I whispered.

His eyes widened and he pushed his lips against mine. I wanted to slap him, but my body betrayed me.

My mouth began to move against his. My lips parted slightly and he slipped the tip of his tongue inside. I pushed back against it with my own. He moaned into my mouth and ground his hips into mine. I gasped. One of his hands traveled down my side and gripped my hip, pulling me tighter against him. I pulled my head back, breaking the kiss, and taking a moment to catch my breath.

"I can't. I can't do this." I shook my head forcing myself to be strong.

William's thumbs brushed over my cheek, wiping away my tears.

"Emma, you are the only person who means anything to me."

Chapter Thirteen

I looked down at my hands and back into his eyes. Heavy raindrops began to fall around us and I shivered at the shift in the weather.

"Come home with me please. I will tell you anything you want to know. Please." He looked terrified and... angry.

The rain got heavier and began to drip down off the branches onto us. Thunder crashed off in the distance. I looked at William and nodded. He quickly wrapped his arm around my waist and pulled me towards his car. The clouds let loose and we were soaked before we made it to the door.

He opened the car door for me and waited for me to get inside before going around to his side. I fastened my seat belt and waited for the awful moment of truths. William started the car and backed out onto the dirt drive that led out of the cemetery. We rode in silence for a moment, listening to the sound of the rain beating against the car.

"Who is she?" I could barely speak. William swallowed hard and shifted gears.

"She... shares a similar... lifestyle with me." He glanced in my direction but quickly looked back at the road.

"What does that mean? Is she a teacher?" I couldn't wrap my head around any of this.

He let out a small choked laugh and shook his head. "No." He looked at me again, his face serious.

It hit me like a brick to the chest. My mind flashed to the third floor. "She's... like me?" I stared off at the rain. How was I so naive to think I was the only one?

"No. No one is like you." He reached over to grab my hand, but I pulled away from him, pressing myself against the car door. "She's like *me*."

I looked over at him, my mouth hanging wide open as I let the information sink in.

"But why would you…" My words trailed off as I tried to understand what he was telling me. He sighed loudly and gripped the steering wheel tighter. His foot pushing down harder on the accelerator.

"Slow down." I dug my fingers into the leather seats as we whipped down the slick streets at frightening speeds.

"She helps me work through things, Emma."

"Work through things? What does that even mean?" I could feel the tears forming again. I wanted so desperately not to cry. For once in my life, I wanted to be the strong one.

"Sexually. She is a… dom." He reached for me again, but I pulled away. His brows pulled together as he watched me recoil from his touch.

"Slow down." My head was spinning and I felt like I was on the verge of dying from a broken heart. None of this made sense.

I wasn't exactly sure of the definition of what a dom was, but I knew William was one. I couldn't begin to picture him giving up all of his control.

"Why was she there?" My patience was gone and I just needed answers. Was she in love with him? Had she come to my aunt's funeral to claim him? The idea made me sick to my stomach. She didn't put up much of a fight, if that was her intention.

"She wasn't there for me. She came to pay her respects to your aunt." He glanced in my direction but quickly looked back at the road. It was pouring harder now and it was almost impossible to see anything. I turned to face him, waiting for him to fill in the blanks.

He licked his lips and continued to explain. "Your aunt…" His voice trailed off as he searched for the right words. My heart was beating out of my chest. He cleared his throat and began again. "You aunt was also like me."

My mouth fell open as I stared at him, wishing the universe would swallow me whole. He knew my aunt. He lied to me.

"No!" I shook my head. "No!"

His hand shot out and grabbed my wrist. "Emma, please! I never touched her. Never! I promise you. I barely knew her." His grip was painfully tight and I tried to pull free. "I haven't been with anyone since I began seeing you."

"You knew her this whole time? You have been lying to me this whole time?" I was seeing red now. My emotions shifted from heartbreak to anger and I wanted to take it out on him.

"Emma, please. I didn't know when I met you. I will tell you anything you want to know." He was looking at me, his eyes full of sadness.

"I hate you!" I seethed. He flinched at my words as if I had actually hit him. I couldn't deal with all of this anymore. With life. "Emma, please." His voice broke. A bright flash flickered across his face and I glanced out of the windshield just in time to see the light grow larger.

"William!" I screamed. His hand ripped away from mine. The sound of my screams was barely audible over the sound of crunching metal and shattering glass. The world spun in circles and I reached out to grab William. My hands thrashed around as I tried desperately to touch him.

As quickly as it happened, everything was still and silent. I was unable to make a sound. I tried to cling to consciousness. My head was lost in a fog. I blinked my eyes open and could see the blurry image of William. He was slumped against the steering wheel, unmoving, with blood on his face. I tried to reach for him, but everything went dim as pain shot through my body; then I knew no more as the darkness descended.

I had no idea how long I was unconscious. It may have been minutes or days. During that time, I dreamed of William. I saw myself back in that grassy patch surrounded by more people I didn't know paying their last respects to Judy.

Fear washed over me at the thought of finally losing William; the only person I had left.

One minute, I'd been ready to throw in the towel on our relationship. Then, all I wanted was to hear was William's voice telling me everything was going to be okay. I didn't care about anything else.

Teresa Mummert

Chapter Fourteen

The steady beeping of the heart monitor machine laced its way through my dreams. It replaced the sound of my text messages. I smiled reading all of the private notes from William.

It beeped and I was back at my aunt's house, hitting snooze on the alarm clock, begging for a few more minutes of sleep.

It beeped and I was in a checkout line at the grocery store. That was probably the least exciting dream I had. Light washed over my face, and that last terrifying second before we crashed played over in my mind. William begging me to stay with him and me telling him I hated him. I felt sick.

Really felt sick. My stomach turned and I slowly blinked my eyes open. My head was

123

throbbing with pain and the slightest amount of illumination magnified it.

"Welcome back," a cheery voice called out. A woman who looked to be in her early forties and wearing cartoon emblazoned scrubs was standing over me, smiling.

"So bright," I whispered, my voice hoarse.

"Sorry about that. How you feeling?" she asked as I continued to blink rapidly.

"William?" I asked, not wanting to waste my voice talking about myself.

"The man you were brought in with? I will have the doctor speak with you about his condition." She leaned in closer to me, brushing my hair from my forehead. Her smile brightened and I nodded, squeezing my eyes closed.

The doctor entered the room right as if on cue. He and the nurse spoke quietly at the foot of my bed.

The doctor moved closer to the head of my bed and was writing something down on a clipboard over me. "How are you feeling Ms. Townsend?"

"My head hurts and I could use a drink."

He continued to write something then paused to speak. "We'll get you some water." He nodded to the nurse and I watched her move to the bedside, and then turned my head slowly back to the doctor.

"William?" I asked urgently.

"We'll know more after some tests. We'll let you know when we do. Right now, he's still unconscious."

"Can you tell me the last thing you remember?" He looked at me expectantly.

"The car accident." My mind flashed to the image of William lying motionless next to me.

"Can you tell me your full name?"

"Emma May Townsend."

"Very good Ms. Townsend. Now, is there someone we can call for you?"

"No." I swallowed hard wanting to fight back my despair. He was all I had now—and I doubted I had him anymore.

I sucked in a deep breath. He was really hurt, and I wasn't there with him. I pushed to sit myself up, but I was dizzy and weak. I reached for the IV in my hand to pull it out. William would need me! I had to go to him.

"Not so fast." The doctor held out his hand to keep me in bed. "Your vitals are stable, but I want to keep you here a little longer just to make sure you are alright. After a CAT scan, we should be able to rule out any serious injury to you. I promise, you can see him then."

I nodded, laying my head back on the pillow. I was too dizzy to stand up anyway.

"How long was I out?" I was afraid to hear the answer.

The doctor checked the watch on his wrist. "Long enough that we're going to be observing you for a bit," the doctor said.

It didn't sound that bad and I wanted to protest. I needed to see William to make sure he was okay.

"Lay back and relax. The test shouldn't take long." Two others in scrubs appeared at my side. I hadn't noticed them before. They locked the railings on my bed and began to push me out of the room.

"I'm fine really. I don't need this." One of the women looked down at me and smiled but no one said anything to me. They were too busy talking amongst themselves using medical jargon that I couldn't begin to understand. I was scared, and I wanted William by my side.

I closed my eyes and forced myself not to cry. I felt like I was dying. Not because of my injuries, but because my heart had been shattered. I had no one else to turn to. I needed to know he was all right.

The test went by in a blur. Everything was normal. I didn't care either way. If William was not okay, I didn't want to live. I was torn between my love and hate for him. I was a mess.

Chapter Fifteen

It seemed like an eternity before I was finally released from the ER. I barely registered the doctor's comments on signs of things to watch for. I just wanted to get to William.

I grabbed my clothing and changed quickly in the tiny restroom. I dared to take a glance at myself in the mirror. I was a mess. My hair was knotted and wild. I ran my hands through my hair and winced as my fingers rubbed over the large lump that had formed after my head bounced off the passenger window. I squeezed my eyes closed and waited a moment for the pain to pass. When it was finally manageable, I turned on the sink and splashed some cold water on my face.

I was suddenly terrified to see William. I didn't know if I could handle seeing him so helpless and broken. The doctor hadn't told me much at all about William yet. He was lucky to be alive, considering he hadn't been wearing his seatbelt at the time. I cringed as the thought of how bad it could have been crossed my mind.

I took a deep breath and forced myself to be strong.

I made my way out into the hallway, glancing in both directions. I spotted a nurses' station down the hall to the right. I made my way toward it, trying not to let my mind run wild with William.

"Excuse me." My voice was shaky and I swallowed hard trying to calm my nerves.

"Yes, ma'am?" The nurse behind the counter looked like she was on the bad end of a long shift.

"I'm looking for William Honor? He was brought in with me." She eyed me for a moment before registering whom I was talking about.

"Yes. He's in 13. Down the hall to the left." She flashed me a quick polite smile and her attention went back to the paperwork she had been filling out. I smiled and turned to find his room. My heart was beating out of my chest and I felt like I was on the verge of a panic attack.

I stood outside of room 13 and took a deep breath. I pushed the door open slowly and slipped inside. The familiar beeping of a heart monitor was in the background. The moment I saw him, my heart sank. He lay in the hospital bed covered in a thin white blanket. I slowly stepped towards his motionless body.

"William?"

He didn't respond and I felt tears threatening to fall. I stepped closer and reached out to touch his hand. All of the emotions of the day came rushing back to me all at once. My aunt's funeral, the mysterious woman, and the accident. My chest ached as I recalled the horrible fight we had just before the crash.

My head began to throb in time with my frantic breathing. I deserved it. I told the man I loved that I hated him and now he lay unconscious. I felt like a monster. I sagged into the chair placed next to the bed for visitors. I suddenly wondered if there had been any other visitors before me. What if that woman showed up here?

Tears pricked my eyes and I used my free hand to dash them away. The lump in my throat was growing and I swallowed hard as I thought about how fucked up my world had become.

I was angry and said things I didn't mean to William, but I was afraid of what other secrets I might uncover. I shook the thought from my head. I had plenty of time to figure out what I would do about our relationship after he woke up. Right now, I just wanted to see his beautiful blue eyes.

He looked peaceful and as if today's events were not weighing heavy on his mind. I was thankful for that. His physical pain would be enough. He didn't need the mental torment on top of it. I squeezed his hand and leaned closer to him.

"I love you, William," I whispered. I had hoped that the words would bring some sort of response from him but he lay perfectly still. Not even a flicker of emotion played on his face. I sighed and lay back in the chair, closing my eyes. How did we come to this point? I was beginning to feel like I was destined to be alone.

I wasn't a religious person. My parents were Christian but we never went to church on Sundays. Part of me wished they had just so I would have someone to turn to in a time like this. I pushed the thought out of my head. If there was a God, he was the one making me suffer.

My mother was a good person. She worked hard and did what she thought was right. That didn't stop my family from being erased from my life by a drunk driver. I shivered at the thought. I wouldn't even allow myself to think of the fact that the drunk driver was my own father.

I could feel the rage bubbling inside of me again. He was a hardworking man, always doing everything he could to make ends meet. His life was stressful and he relieved that stress by unwinding with a bottle of Jack. I didn't blame him. No matter how hard he tried, something always went wrong. My mother didn't understand. She would fight with him about never being around. The fights would escalate out of control at times. She should have listened to him when he told her to stop. She never listened to him. He was good man, deep down. He treated me like a princess, never mean or cold like he was to my mother. It was because I listened to him. She pushed him over the edge. After they would fight, he would leave for hours at a time. If she would have just listened, he would have been around more.

The night of the accident, they had argued for about an hour. I remember sitting on the couch and flipping through the channels on the television, doing my best to block them out. My father grabbed his keys to leave again, as he always did. Taking a swig from his nearly empty bottle of Jack, he pushed past my mother and made his way to the car. My mother ran after him and jumped in the passenger side. She was determined to force him to spend time with her. That was the last time I saw them alive.

I wanted to escape, run away from everything. That is what I did after my parents passed away and look what it got me. Not that I had a choice. I was forced to live with my aunt even though it was obvious I could have done a better job on my own.

Teresa Mummert

Chapter Sixteen

The door to William's room squeaked open and I quickly wiped away my tears. A doctor stepped in, glancing over a clipboard in his hands. His eyes caught mine and he gave me a sympathetic smile.

"I'm Doctor Johnson. You're his next of kin?"

I thought quickly. "I'm his fiancé," I said.

"We need to take William here for some tests. His first scans show some swelling and a subdural hematoma. He also has some cracked ribs and mild abrasions. We need to repeat the CAT scan to see about his head injury," he explained. "After that, we'll get him up and into a room of his own."

I nodded and tried to smile politely at him, swiping a tear from my cheek. I glanced over at William before forcing myself to release his hand.

A nurse and orderly were soon at the doctor's side and they began pushing William's bed from the room. I stood, not sure if my heart could take the separation, but my feet wouldn't allow me to follow. Not that I would have been allowed to go with him.

I glanced around the room. There was another bed on the far side. I made my way to it and climbed in. I need to rest my eyes. Really, I needed to break down while I had a moment alone. I snuggled my face into the pillow and began to sob.

I had no idea where I should go with my life now. The thought of going back to my aunt's house made me sick. I didn't know if William was going to be okay and if he would even want me around. I wasn't even sure if I wanted to be around. Everything was just... wrong now. The few friends I had were off on vacation celebrating their new lives, and I lay crying, alone. I sobbed harder, burying my face in the stark white pillow.

After a while, I had run out of tears to cry. I was drained and didn't want to think about the day's events. I drifted off, burying my overwhelming sadness in sleep.

When I awoke, William's bed was back beside mine. I jumped up and rushed to his side. He was still sleeping peacefully. I ran my hand over a bandage near his temple. The tears began to prick my eyes again and I shook my head, forcing myself to be strong.

A nurse entered the room and tilted her head towards me. She was carrying a tray of food. My stomach growled at the smell of it.

"I thought you might be hungry." She smiled and sat the tray on the cart next to me.

I gave her a small smile in return. "Thank you."

She nodded and walked towards the machines to check William's vitals.

"Is he... okay?" I was terrified to hear the answer.

"His tests look good." She paused. "Are you related to Mr. Honor?"

I swallowed hard, hoping she wasn't about to kick me out of his room.

"He is my fiancé," I said again, since this was a different nurse. I pulled my hands down to my lap when she tried to check my hand for a ring. "We just got engaged." I smiled weakly. "He doesn't have anyone one else here," I added hoping that would convince her. She nodded.

"The doctor can explain his injuries; he'll be in to see you in a bit, and we'll be moving Mr. Honor upstairs to a room."

I nodded and wiped at my eyes. All of this was too much to absorb.

"You should eat something," she said quietly and turned to leave the room.

I lifted the lid off the plate of food. It was mashed potatoes and some sort of turkey gravy mixture. I was starving. I began to slowly eat as something began to vibrate on the far side of his bed. Curious, I began to search for the noise. I opened the closet door and dug through a small bag in the bottom.

Inside was William's clothing, his wallet and cell phone. The phone continued to buzz and the screen flashed. The caller I.D. said 'A'. I held it to my chest for a moment, deciding whether or not to answer. Before I could make up my mind, it stopped. I let out the breath I had been holding.

Suddenly, it chirped with a new voicemail, causing me to jump in shock. I bit my lip as I wiped at the screen. I looked back at William and hit the button to listen.

I placed my finger over my open ear to block out the sound of the beeping. I stared at William's stilled body as the message began to play.

"William, it's me," A silky voice purred from the other end of the line. My heart leapt into my throat. Who was this woman? "I'm sorry about earlier. I had no idea you would be there... with her." My blood was boiling. It was Allison from the funeral. I wanted to jump through the phone and strangle her. "Anyway, I just wanted to say I'm sorry. I'd like it if you stopped by the club. Maybe I could let you take out some of your anger on me?" She laughed quietly and I squeezed my eyes closed. It cut through me like a knife.

The message ended and I blinked several times, pushing the tears back once again. I looked over at William, the fire inside me reignited. I wanted to scream at him, but he lay perfectly still.

I glanced down at the phone, pondering whether or not I should throw it against the wall.

It seemed like an eternity before the doctor came back into the room. I looked at him expectantly, waiting to see why William hadn't woken up.

"Mr. Honor suffered a severe concussion. Right now, he is in a medically induced coma so the swelling in his brain can reduce. He has a subdural hemotoma. Basically, a bleeding bruise in his skull. We have given him a drug called Mannitol for the intracranial pressure. His CAT scan and MRI results look promising, but for now, we just need to keep an eye on him. He'll be unconscious until the swelling goes down. At best, he'll be here at least a week. Does he have any family?"

I nodded. "I'll contact them," I said quietly.

The doctor nodded after a final check on William, and left the room, leaving me alone with him.

Should I call his parents? I knew he was not on good terms with his father, but his mother cared deeply about him. That much was obvious. I bit my lip as I glanced back to William.

He may hate me to wake and find his father here, if he even came, but it would pale in comparison to the anger I felt right now. There was still no guarantee that he would even wake. I pushed the thought from my mind.

I had to call them. My stomach was in knots. I began to search William's contact list. It strangely had mostly just letters of the alphabet. I continued to scroll and found a contact labeled 'mine'. I clicked it and my number appeared. I smiled, breathing a sigh of relief that it wasn't someone else. I scrolled further and found 'mother'. I took a few calming breaths before clicking the call button.

It rang several times before it clicked and a woman's voice filled my ears.

"Hello, sweet boy." It was his mother. I swallowed hard.

"This is Emma." She was silent for a moment.

"How are you dear? Is everything okay?" Her voice grew concerned with each word.

"There was an accident."

I explained everything to Mrs. Honor, leaving out the other woman at my aunt's funeral and the big fight we had had just before the crash. She assured me she would be on the next flight out. His father, however, may not be able to make it.

I had to bite my tongue to keep from saying anything about him. My nerves suddenly took over as I thought of being face to face with his parents again. Without him, it was libel to get very hard to deal with. His mother was kind and I knew she wouldn't be a problem.

I sat back down on the chair next to William's bed and ate the food. For a hospital, it was surprisingly good and I ate every bite.

People passed the room and I could hear them laughing and giggling. I wasn't sure I'd ever be able to smile again. I felt empty, and even though William was at my side, he offered no comfort for my sadness.

A knock came at the door, jarring me from my pity party.

"If you're finished with your tray," a young man held out his hand. I nodded and he grabbed it, turning to leave as quickly as possible.

I sighed and looked over my surroundings. It seemed like forever before he was moved to a room. I grabbed the remote off the stand beside me and flipped through channels. It was going to be the longest week of my life.

Chapter Seventeen

The next day, I was waiting for William's parents to arrive. I was scared his father would show, but I knew it would mean something to William to wake and see both of his parents.

I wiped my clammy palms over my jeans as William's phone rang to life. The caller I.D. read 'mother'. I answered it, trying hard to sound cheery and positive.

"We've just landed, dear. We should arrive in an hour or so." She said 'we'. My heart sank.

"Great. I look forward to seeing you." I was lying. It's not that I didn't want them to come; I just didn't want to deal with that asshole while dealing with all of this.

I paced the floor for a bit, then finally, exhausted, sat down.

When the door cracked open almost an hour later, I felt my heart seize.

"Good news. The swelling appears to have subsided and we may be able to wake your fiancé soon enough." The nurse beamed at me and I smiled back, wanting to jump for joy.

"Thank you!" I clasp my hands over my mouth to keep from shrieking. Just as I began to forget my nerves, the door pushed open wider. In walked William's parents. His father was mumbling something about the substandard conditions of the hospital and Mrs. Honor looked sad. Her eyes were swollen and red like she had been crying the entire flight.

Gerald eyed me while he entered the room but didn't say anything.

"Oh... sweet dear! How is my son?" Martha asked as her hands rested on either side of my face.

"He is doing much better. They think he is well enough to wake... soon." I smiled as she pulled me in for a hug. It was awkward hugging someone I barely knew, but it felt good to be held. I let my arms slink around her back and squeezed her to me.

"So, what did he do this time?" Gerald sneered and glanced over at the bed.

"It was an accident." I sniffed as I tried not to let my emotions take over. It would be too easy to take my frustrations out on his father. I was having a hard time containing my emotions. William was the one person who could make me feel in control when I was absolutely powerless. Now, I felt lost.

A doctor entered the room and turned his attention to Gerald. Martha looped her arm in mine and tugged me towards the door.

"Come on, dear. Let's let the men talk." She smiled up at me. I was hesitant to follow. I wanted to know what was going on and man or not, I deserved to know. She patted my arm and I let her pull me out into the hall. We made our way to the elevator and waited for the doors to open.

"I can't leave him." I said, taking a step back.

"We aren't going anywhere. I just want to grab us a bite to eat. You must be starving." She smiled and the doors slid open. I placed my hand over my stomach. I really could use something to eat. I stepped inside.

We made our way to the lobby and I glanced over the sign to find directions to the cafeteria.

"This way." Martha tugged me in the direction of the food. I was grateful to have a mother figure around. We stood in line and ordered our meals.

"I'm really worried," I confessed. Martha glanced over at me and picked up a bottle of tea.

"No need to worry. William is strong, just like his father."

I flinched. "They don't seem like they are anything alike."

She looked over at me, her eyebrow raised. She didn't say anything and I wished I had never opened my mouth. William hated his father and I was certain the feeling was mutual. Even I couldn't deny that they both seemed to love power. Still, William was really caring when you got to know him. I couldn't picture Gerald being affectionate.

We made our way to a table in the back corner of the room. Martha gestured for me to sit and I did. She slid in a seat across from me as awkward silence filled the room.

"He's not so bad, you know? Gerald..." Martha said, shaking her head as she unwrapped her sandwich. I had the sudden realization that I was staring into my future. Is this what I had to look forward to if I stayed with William? A controlling, cold and cruel man? No... she was wrong.

I took a bite of my food and grabbed a little orange pill bottle from my purse. I pushed down on the lid and dumped one of the small white ovals into my hand.

"You in a lot of pain, dear?" Martha asked, cocking her head to the side.

"A little," I shrugged as I popped the pill in my mouth and took a drink. It was awkward sitting across from my possibly ex-boyfriend's mother. I couldn't think of anything to say. I knew he blamed his father for many things, but in my eyes, his mother was just as responsible for his unhappiness. Why didn't she try to protect him from him? Why did I care? William wasn't mine anymore.

"You know, sometimes emotional pain can manifest itself into physical pain. They say depression can actually hurt." She took another bite of her sandwich and made a face of disgust at the sub-par meal.

What the fuck was she talking about?

"I'm pretty sure my headache is a direct result of my head bouncing off a car window." I didn't mean to sound snippy, but I couldn't help it. Everything in my life was just wrong. I was angry and bitter.

"Of course it is. I didn't mean to offend. I just... I know a relationship... can be difficult." She was assuming my relationship with William was like hers.

I sighed, feeling like the biggest jerk on the planet. She hadn't done anything to me. She was scared for the wellbeing of her son and here I was, having an attitude with her. "I'm sorry. It has been a long week."

She waved it off and we both ate for a few moments in silence.

"You're good for him," she said as she picked up her drink and took a long sip. I pulled my eyebrows together as I watched her. "I know how he can be, but you're still here. That says something about the kind of woman you are."

I smiled slightly. It felt good that we had someone's approval, even if it was at the end of our relationship.

"Come on, dear. Let's go see what the doctor has to say." She stood and waited for me to gather my things. I dumped them in the trashcan and held open the door for her to leave the cafeteria.

The ride up the elevator was the longest of my life. I couldn't handle the stress of not knowing if he was going to be okay. I hated him, but I missed him.

We reached the room just as the doctor was leaving. Gerald was running his hand through his hair as he watched us enter. He gave me a quick glance and turned his attention to his wife. It was obvious I hadn't won his approval. I rolled my eyes without thinking. I glanced back up to see his glare as his muscles flexed over his jaw. I swallowed hard and made my way to the seat next to William.

"Any news?" Martha asked, regaining Gerald's attention.

"These doctors are incompetent. I'll make a few phone calls and see if I can't get a real specialist in here." Martha lovingly stroked Gerald's arm in an attempt to soothe him.

I turned to William and slipped my fingers into his. Tears pricked my eyes and I closed them tightly, pleading with myself not to break down and show weakness in front of his father.

"I'll make arrangements for a hotel," he said as he pulled out his phone and headed into the hallway. Martha came to join me at William's side.

"He looks so peaceful." She placed a hand on his leg and smiled. I sniffed as I stared at his face.

"I booked us a suite over at the Plaza. Let's go get settled in," Gerald announced, not bothering to reenter the room. Martha shot me a small smile and turned to join her husband.

"You take care of my boy, Emma," she called over her shoulder before she disappeared, leaving me alone with my thoughts.

His own parents didn't bother sticking around to make sure he was even okay. Sure, they would call some doctors, but that paled in comparison to being by his side when... *if* he woke.

Chapter Eighteen

The next two days were the longest and loneliest days of my life. William's parents stopped by from time to time, but it was always on their way to somewhere else.

The new doctor they had had flown in took over William's case with expert care. I was thankful and it was a great relief to know that he was in the best hands possible.

William's parents only stayed in town for another day. Gerald had a new movie that would begin filming soon. I couldn't imagine how anything could be more important than your own child's life.

I never left his side. I felt lost without him. Day and night I stayed by him, pleading with him to get better. Finally, the day had come that William's condition had improved significantly and they would be allowing him to wake up. I used all of the samples and trials I could find to make myself look half-decent as I waited for him to regain consciousness. The hospital bathroom was less than luxurious but I made it work.

The first time I looked into his beautiful deep blue eyes, my heart was beating out of my chest. He squeezed his eyes closed and looked around, adjusting to the light. I shifted my weight nervously from one foot to the other. I didn't know if he even wanted me around after the argument we'd had.

The doctor checked William's vitals as I held his hand.

"Where am I?" he asked as he ran his hand though his hair and down over his face that was no longer clean-shaven.

"Kippling Hospital." My voice cracked as he eyed me, his eyebrows pulled together. I shoved my hands in my back pockets as I chewed on my lip.

"Welcome back to the world," the doctor said cheerily. William smiled and winced like he was in pain. "Can you tell me your name?"

"William... Honor." He groaned as he rubbed his head. The doctor scribbled a note on his paper.

"Great. Can you tell me the last thing you remember?" He stared at William, pen in hand.

"Ughh... yeah, sure..." His eyes darted to me and then back to the doctor. "I remember... shit..." He pinched the bridge of his nose with his fingers.

"It's okay." The doctor patted him on the arm. "You've been through a serious trauma. It may take a little while to come back to you. In the meantime, we will do our best to keep you comfortable."

William squeezed his eyes shut.

"What happened?" William asked.

"You were in a car accident. You're very lucky to be alive. You and Emma." The doctor glanced at me. "I'll give you two a minute." The doctor turned and left the room. He had warned me that William may not remember the accident, but he assured me that it would most likely be temporary. Head injuries were tricky, though, and they couldn't guarantee me anything.

I pulled my hands from my pockets and began to wring them together. I was afraid to look William in the eye.

"William…" my voice trailed off.

"Call me Will." He pushed himself up into a sitting position and raised the bed to meet his back. I cringed at the nickname. That is what his ex-wife used to call him. I wondered if he remembered her, but I was too scared to ask.

"Will… ugh… Do you remember me?" I stole a glance in his direction. His eyebrows furrowed as he tried to place me. Tears began to cloud my sight and a swallowed, struggling to push the lump from my throat.

I nodded, knowing the answer. A tear fell down my cheek and I wanted to turn and run away but my feet refused to cooperate.

"Hey, don't cry. Come here." He motioned for me to come closer to him. I sat down on the edge of his bed and he wrapped his arms around me and pulled me into his chest. "Shh…" he whispered into my hair as his hand rubbed my back. I held on to him as tight as I could, and let my tears flow freely onto his hospital gown.

"You said you would never forget me," I sobbed.

He didn't hold me as if I was his lover. He held me like a stranger comforting a crying child. I felt like an idiot and more importantly, I felt alone. Maybe this was better. I was ready to leave him, now he didn't know who I was. My heart was crushed. I got exactly what I deserved. I pulled back from him, placing my hand on his chest. He used his hands to push the hair from my face. His stormy blue eyes searched mine as his heart began to beat double time under my fingers. I looked at his chest then back to him. Hoping. The doctor rounded the corner with his clipboard, followed by a nurse holding some sort of medicine.

"Well, looks like you two have been getting reacquainted." He smiled in my direction but I avoided his gaze and slid off the bed. I backed against the wall as the nurse slid between us and began checking his vitals and gave him the small plastic cup of pills in her hand. The doctor spouted off some information, but I didn't absorb any of it. My brain was in a fog of sadness.

It took a minute for me to realize the room had fallen silent. I glanced up to see all three sets of eyes on me.

"I'm sorry?" I said, hoping they would repeat the information.

"You will be helping him with his transition at home, correct?"

William's parents had skipped town for what they deemed as more important things and that only left me. The complete stranger with the broken heart. This should be fun. I wiped the tears from my cheek and nodded. He gave me a small smile and turned back to William.

"Good. All looks well and we should be able to have you out of here in no time." He smiled again and William thanked him. Soon, we were alone again and the walls felt as if they were closing in on us.

I made myself busy by gathering my things. I dug through my purse and located my keys.

Thankfully William's... Will's parents had thought ahead and retrieved my car from the pizza joint I had left it at lifetime ago. Back when I still had a life to speak of.

If I thought I was empty before meeting William, it didn't hold a candle to the aching I felt inside now. The worst part was that I would have to stay by his side and smile at his empty eyes, keeping my pain and sadness to myself. I wanted to scream at him, to tell him everything he had done to me, but I couldn't. He had a fresh slate, even if it was temporary. This would be the best time for me to leave. When he had no idea that the person he loved was walking out on him. I laughed at myself as my eyes blurred with tears. What was I thinking? How could I walk away from him? He was all I had and I loved him. When I thought I might lose him, I didn't want to go on myself.

I hated myself for wanting to stay and I hated myself for wanting to abandon him. There was no winning in this situation. I was destined to suffer in sadness. If he remembered, maybe then I would confront him and tell him how hurt I was, but would it matter?

The nurse brought us two trays of food and we sat together in awkward silence. I wanted to probe him further, find out what memories he retained, but I couldn't bring myself to do it. If he remembered any woman and not me, it would be the final stab to the heart. I couldn't take anymore.

I pushed the Salisbury steak around my plate as I watched him devour his food.

"You should eat something." He smiled as he spoke and a mixture of anger and longing bubbled up inside of me. I cut a small bite and ate it. He smiled again and turned back to his food. His kindness and pleasant demeanor confused me even more. His brain had taken him to more pleasant times. Times that didn't include me. That hurt.

We finished our meal and only had to deal with doctors a few more times before it was time to get some sleep. I curled up in the small plush chair that offered little in the way of comfort.

"Emma..." William's voice trailed off and I didn't ask him to continue his thought.

"Good night," I whispered and tucked my knees into my chest, allowing exhaustion to win its battle it had fought with me over the past few days.

The next morning could not arrive soon enough. Doctors and nurses floated in and out and eventually they had given us the go ahead to leave the hospital.

I told myself I would drop off William and leave, go back to my aunt's. I assumed I'd be allowed back in the house by now. The thought terrified me, but the thought of being with William, and him not even knowing who I was, was worse.

I stole glances at him as he stared out the window, taking in the unfamiliar surroundings.

"Not much farther." I turned down the road towards his place. He looked confused and my heart sank. He needed me. I needed to be there for him.

Chapter Nineteen

As we stepped inside the expansive building, William looked around.

"This is ours?" He asked as he looked over towards the stairs. I smiled and looked down at my feet.

"This is yours. I live... somewhere else." The thought of my aunt stung. I didn't know how I would ever go back to that place. I didn't want to.

He looked at me for a moment before walking towards the steps. I followed behind him. He paused at the door on the next landing.

"This it?" he asked. I nodded. His eyes traveled up the next set of stairs. "What's up there?" I couldn't contain the blush that spread across my face.

"It's under construction." I lied, feeling the guilt wash over me. As much as I had enjoyed our time on the third floor, I still had no idea where William and I stood. I was in no hurry to bring back the guy who had broken my heart.

He ran his hand through his hair and stepped aside, waiting for me to unlock the door. I did, with the key he had made for me. I would have to remember to return it when he got his memory back. I pushed the door open so he could step inside. He looked around, taking it all in before stepping aside so I could enter.

"What do you think?" I asked, dropping my purse on the island. His eyes followed me as I opened the fridge for a drink.

"Want something?" I asked as I grabbed a soda. His eyes flicked to the island where he kept his extra bottles of liquor and back to me. My brows pulled together as I waited for him to tell me he remembered something.

"A soda would be fine." He grinned. He looked so relaxed, so carefree. I didn't want to go back to the fight before the accident. It was easier to lie to myself and pretend that this was the man wasn't the one who had broken my heart. I wasn't sure that was even possible.

I grabbed him a drink from the fridge and sat it on the island. He walked towards me and stopped, grabbing his drink.

"Thank you." His half grin revealed a sexy dimple that made my whole body go warm.

"You're welcome."

He ran a hand through his hair and cracked open his drink. I rummaged through the fridge for something to eat.

"You seem to know your way around here." He cocked his head to the side. My mind automatically wondered who else knew their way around his place.

"I've spent a lot of time here." I bit my lip as I grabbed a few things from the fridge to make sandwiches. I laid everything on the counter in front of us and grabbed a few plates from the cupboard and a knife from the drawer.

He took another sip from his drink as he watched me begin to slice a tomato.

"You are doing that all wrong." He rounded the counter and stood behind me with his body flush against my back. His arms came around me as he slid his hands over mine and guided the knife. His breath blew against my neck causing my skin to break out in goose bumps. I stiffened, not sure if I could handle having him so near. "There," he whispered against my ear.

"I see you didn't forget everything." I laughed nervously. I was terrified to deal with all of the secrets and lies. He backed away.

"I guess some things just stay with you." He smiled as he took a seat on the stool in front of me. My heart ached. I wasn't one of those things. Maybe Allison was. As scared as I was to deal with our problems, it hurt that he could forget who I was. I wanted to lash out, but it would be pointless. I wiped at my check quickly and ducked my head, finishing our sandwiches. I could feel his eyes on me the entire time but I forced myself not to look at him. I would completely lose it if I had to stare into those damn blue eyes that were void of all memory of me. One thing I had noticed was his lack of... firmness against me. Was the gesture completely innocent? I snorted at using the word innocent to describe William. He looked at me as if I was completely crazy.

"Sorry. I just thought of something... funny." I slid his plate in front of him and took a seat next to him. It was awkward being so close to him without the sexual tension that usually pulled us together. I picked at the roll of my sandwich as he took several large bites of his.

"Not hungry?" he asked as he shoved more food in his mouth. I shrugged as I watched him devour his food.

"You should really eat something." He sounded concerned, not his normal bossy self. I picked up my sandwich and began to eat. He smiled at me and took his plate to the sink. I grinned to myself as I took a few more bites. This was going to take some getting used to. I didn't know if I was capable of just being a friend to him.

My purse began to vibrate on the counter in front of me. I fished around inside and grabbed my phone. It wasn't mine. I dropped it and dug further. I grabbed William's phone and glanced at the screen. The caller I.D. read 'A'. I glared at the phone and hit ignore, dropping it back into my back. I sighed as

William turned around. I needed to get away from here as soon as I could.

"Finished?" He gestured towards my plate. I nodded and let him take it to the sink. I hated that I was so mad at him for lying and now I was the one lying to him. I should have handed him the phone. Let him see how he had hurt me. I didn't. I was a coward.

"What are you thinking about?" he asked as he glanced over his shoulder at me.

"Just been a long week." I sighed and let my shoulders sag. He rounded the island and put his hands on my shoulders. He began to rub small circles with his thumbs.

"I'm sorry I put you through all of this. I don't know what I did to deserve your kindness." He chuckled softly. "I really don't."

I laughed and let myself relax. *Nothing.* He didn't deserve to have me here right now.

"Come on. Why don't you show me around."

I pushed back and stood glancing around the place. "Well, this is the kitchen and the living room." I made sweeping gesture with my hands. I walked across the floor to the bathroom. "This is self-explanatory." He was right behind me. I turned around and tried to duck passed him without rubbing against his chest. He smiled as I walked him to another door and pushed it open. "This is your bedroom." I glanced down at the floor as he walked past me and looked around.

The room was still littered with my belongings. He walked to the foot of the bed and picked up a small scrap of yellow fabric.

I blushed and grabbed my torn panties from his hand, hiding them behind my back. A grin spread across his face and he laughed deep in his chest.

"I guess you know this room pretty well."

"Who said they were mine?" I raised my eyebrow at him that only made him laugh harder.

"I sure hope they're not mine," he joked. I laughed and looked down at the floor. At least in this state he assumed he was a one-woman man. He ran his hands through his hair as he eyed the bed.

"I'm actually pretty tired." He gripped his T-shirt and pulled it over his head. His chest was rock hard and I had the urge to cross the room and wrap my arms around him but I had to remind myself that things were not the same as they were a week ago. I was still hurting and William still had no idea who I was.

"I'll let you get some rest." I turned to leave but his hand caught my wrist, sending my pulse racing into overdrive.

"Stay," he whispered. I turned slowly to face him. He seemed to take notice of my pulse and released my arm. My heart was broken and if it hadn't been for the accident I would be miles away right now, cursing his name.

"I just want to sleep," he reassured me. I bit my lip and his eyes narrowed. For a second I saw the old William. I quickly released it from my teeth as he undid his belt and slid his jeans down.

I slipped off my shoes and began to undo my pants, feeling suddenly shy. He turned to crawl into the bed, giving me some privacy. I opted to leave on my tank and underwear, not wanting to encourage him. I slipped under the covers behind him and turned away from his body. The bed shifted under his weight as he rolled over and wrapped his muscular arms around me. He snuggled his face into my neck and inhaled deeply. His hands never moved and after a few minutes, his breathing grew deeper. I knew he had finally fallen asleep. I need this, I told myself. I deserved a little comfort after what I had gone through recently. I sighed and let my eyes close, giving in to exhaustion.

Chapter Twenty

I awoke in a tangled mess of limbs. William held me firmly against his body. I wiggled to free myself from his grip, but that caused something inside of him to awaken and he ground his hips into my backside, letting out a deep moan in my ear. I tried to pry his hands from my waist but his grip tightened and one of his hands trailed to my hip, gripping it firmly. My breathing grew unsteady and I knew if I didn't get free from him soon I wouldn't have will power. Will Power I laughed to myself. If he was ever a porn star that would suit him perfectly.

"William," I whispered, but he didn't respond. I reached over my shoulder and pushed against his chest. He squeezed tighter as his hips rubbed harder against me. "Stop it!" I struggled again to free my body and in a flash I was underneath him, my arms pinned above my head. William was struggling to catch his breath as he stared down at me. After a few deep breaths, he finally registered my look of anger and raised his body from mine.

"I'm sorry," he said as he ran his hand through his messy hair. He backed his body off mine and collapsed beside me.

"It's fine." I sat up and quickly scanned the room for my jeans. I found them and began pulling them on as quickly as possible. He was sitting up as I buttoned them. What was I thinking? I really thought sleeping in the same bed with him wouldn't end up this way?

"We don't have a very... happy relationship I take it?" His eyes were on mine and I felt the increasing urge to flee. I couldn't find the words to let him know exactly what I was feeling so, frustrated, I pulled my fingers through my knotted mess of hair and left the room.

I made my way to the kitchen to make a pot of coffee and rethink my plan to stay with him. He was fine now and outside of forgetting a few things, he seemed able to take care of himself. His hands rested on my shoulders and I jumped. I didn't hear him come up behind me. He backed away at my reaction.

"I'm sorry." He looked down at the ground before walking over to a cabinet and grabbing two coffee mugs. The only thing he seemed not to remember was me. My heart sank. I needed to get out of here as soon as possible.

I turned to fill our cups, careful not to stare at his naked chest as I poured. I found the sugar and dumped a healthy dose into my mug. I sat it down on the island and began to sip it slowly.

"Whatever I did to you... I'm sorry."

I rolled my eyes at him. "You don't even remember what you're apologizing for."

His face grew serious as he pondered that. "I hope I never remember. I don't want to be that person." He took another long sip from his mug.

I felt like the worst person in the world making him suffer for something he didn't know he did, but I didn't know if I could forgive him. Memory loss or not, it was him who lied to me and... possibly cheated on me. I swallowed the lump in my throat.

"You weren't the person I thought you were." All of the events of the past few days played through my head. I wanted to scream at him, to throw it in his face, but I just couldn't. He had been through enough. Even so, I couldn't forget that any of it happened.

"I need to go home today." I tried to keep my tone cheery. He didn't say anything.

"You won't have a car. You can call me if you need anything." I let my voice trail off. He sat his mug down with a strong thud and made his way back to his bedroom. He slammed the door loudly and I jumped, spilling my coffee.

"Shit!" I muttered as I grabbed the dishrag and cleaned the spill. I wanted to go after him. I was dying to wrap my arms around him and tell him I loved him. Instead, I threw the washcloth into the sink, grabbed my purse, and placed his phone on the counter. I looked around one last time before leaving the apartment.

Chapter Twenty-One

I was terrified to go back to my aunt's house. I didn't want to ever step foot inside of that place again, but I had nowhere else to go. I needed to take some time to deal with her death before figuring out what I want for the rest of my life.

The house was dark and quiet, which was not unusual, but now it felt so much emptier. I threw my purse on the table. I rummaged through the fridge for something hard to drink. I needed to forget.

I grabbed a bottle of cheap vodka from the shelf and a bottle of ice tea. I took several shots in quick succession before settling on the couch and finding an old rerun to watch. I glanced up at the pictures hung on the wall of Judy and my mother.

It wasn't long before the warmth of the alcohol took over my body. I curled up in a ball and began to sob quietly until sleep took over my body.

My dream immediately went back to that moment in the cemetery.

I glanced over my shoulder looking for William. I find him in the arms of Allison. My heart cracks into a thousand jagged shards as he sweeps her into his embrace. I try to run for him, to scream his name but I can't make a sound. I am forced to watch him locked in a loving embrace with this evil woman.

I sat straight up, sweat dampening my skin. I pushed my hair from my forehead, and tried desperately to steady my breathing. I stumbled into the kitchen in a daze, and grabbed the bottle of vodka from the fridge, taking a long pull from the bottle before coming up for air. I slumped into the chair at the kitchen table, bottle still in hand, as I gazed down the hallway.

I wanted someone, anyone to make me feel like I wasn't completely alone in this world. I had no one. The man I had fallen in love with broke my heart and no longer remembered what we had in the first place. I was exhausted, emotionally as well as physically. I didn't want to try anymore. Everything I touch broke. I let William into my heart and that had crumbled as well. I was cursed.

I took another drink from the bottle and sat it back in the fridge. I curled up on the couch and cried myself back to sleep.

When morning finally came, my head throbbed almost as much as my heart. I had no purpose. No class to attend. No job to fill the lonely empty hours. I was locked in emotional torment. My own personal hell. I let myself get caught up in William. His dangerous devil-may-care attitude. I allowed myself to throw caution to the wind. That wind turned out to be a tornado, sweeping me up in it until it was done toying with me before slamming me back to earth.

I trudged into the kitchen and began scanning the fridge for something to eat. I began preparing a fresh pot of coffee, which reminded me of William. Of course it did. Everything reminded me of him. He was all-consuming.

I decided on some frozen waffles. I needed to put something in my stomach besides liquor. Maybe later I could go to the store and stock the cupboards with some of the things I like. I still had a small amount of cash tucked away from the death of my parents. I didn't like to use it. It was a nice cushion for a rainy day. That day had finally come.

I sat down and absentmindedly stabbed at my food with my fork. Maybe I could plan a trip to Michigan and just get away from this place for a while. All of my friends would be long gone, off to start their new lives after college. I sighed and took a small bite of my food.

My purse began to ring and I stuck my hand inside to fish out my phone. My stomach twisted in knots as I read the caller I.D. William the Conqueror flashed on the screen. I wanted to ignore him, but he may need my help. Reluctantly I swallowed my bite and answered the phone.

"Hey," William's voice was quiet and something seemed to be bothering him.

"Hey," I replied, my voice cracking. "Everything okay?" I tried to force myself to sound chipper.

"Yeah, I guess. Just lonely around here. I was wondering if maybe you wanted to come by. We could go out for dinner or..." His voice trailed off and I realized I had been holding my breath.

"I have a lot of things to do today." I looked around my empty place. Tears stung at my eyes and I squeezed them closed.

He sighed heavily into the receiver.

"Alright, I understand. I'm supposed to meet up with some woman later anyway. Angela I think her name was."

I didn't know it was possible for my heart to ache any more than it already was. I felt like I might actually die from a broken heart.

"You can't!" My words came out more frantic than I intended. I took a deep breath and tried to sound more casual.

"She is your ex-girlfriend. You just… can't."

"My ex?"

"Someone you used to sleep with. You told her it was over and she wouldn't accept it." I sighed.

He laughed a little. "That explains why she was such a bitch."

I laughed at his response and we both sat in silence for a moment.

"I won't see her, Emma."

I nodded to myself as the tears began to slide down my cheeks.

"I don't want to keep you."

He sounded as sad as I felt. I knew he was lonely and I should tell him he could go see whomever he wants. I couldn't force myself to do it. Angela was no good for him and she would undoubtedly take full advantage of his weakened state.

"Bye, William." I clicked the end call button before he responded. I told myself he would be fine without me. I didn't know how I would be without him, but that didn't matter anymore. No matter what he says or does now, he is still that same man I had fought with. He was hiding secrets from me. Secrets he couldn't even recall. There were too many what ifs. I sat my fork down, my appetite completely lost.

Gut-wrenching sobs took over me as I let everything I had been feeling take over me completely. I was lost. William haunted my every thought and I was still unable to let my self grieve over my aunt. It was all too real. Her things sat just down the hall, untouched. I was afraid even to open the door as if she would still be there, only not there at all.

I grabbed a change of clothes from my bedroom and made my way into the bathroom. I needed a long hot shower to ease my mind. My tears mixed with the shower water as I scrubbed my body clean. I wiped away his scent from my skin, the lingering touch of his fingertips. I felt defeated. When the tears finally stopped coming I turned off the water and walked to my bedroom, and grabbed a tank top and a pair of jean shorts. I dressed quickly, not wanting to spend any more time back that hall than I needed to. I glanced across the hall to her room.

I picked up a book from the top of my dresser. I had read it a five times before, a western romance. The pages where torn and the spine cracked. I traipsed to the living room and began reading it again from the beginning. I knew if I stuck to it, it would be time for bed when I finished. Anything to make the time pass.

I tried to concentrate on the story that I already knew by heart, but I couldn't stop thinking of *him.* I wanted answers. I wanted to know what he did with that woman and when. Not even he could answer my questions. I wish I had someone to talk to.

Maybe one day. Maybe if his memory returns he could tell me. I shook my head and flipped the page, my vision becoming to blurred by tears to make out the words on the page.

I looked over at the kitchen table, wondering if I should call him. He would have no problem comforting me. He would listen to me ramble on about my aunt and how much I missed her. I didn't allow myself to give in to my impulses. I needed to forget him. It was a silly fling. All the talks of marriage and love where just part of the fantasy. In reality, William was a very sexy man with lots of money. He didn't need me. I was damaged goods. I was needy and self-destructive.

My aunt. What did he mean that she was 'like him'? She was cold and uncaring, sure, but not the type of person I could see strapping someone down on a device and spanking them. Oh, god. She knew him. She knew my William. I swallowed hard. He wasn't mine anymore and who knew how many other women called him theirs. I felt like I was going to be sick.

Too many unanswered questions. I turned back to my book and began to read, forcing myself to fall into the love story about a cattle rancher and the daughter of a wealthy banker.

Chapter Twenty-Two

I felt like I was trapped in the movie *Groundhog's Day*. One day ran into the next. It didn't help that I had begun to use alcohol again to numb the pain. It only helped temporarily; sometimes all it did was magnify my sadness.

I prepared myself some coffee and a boring breakfast while I stared at my phone, hoping that at least I could hear William's voice. He didn't call. Perhaps he finally regained his memory and realized I wasn't the one he had wanted. That all of this was a sick game to seduce me and have me at his every beck and call. I shuttered at the thought.

Deep down, I'd believed William when he told me he loved me. I knew he wasn't the picture perfect ideal man for most, but I loved him.

My nearly nonexistent appetite disappeared once again. If anything good was going to come of this, at least I would have a decent figure. How William ever looked at me like I was perfect, I would never understand. Perhaps he was a better liar than I realized.

I made my way to the shower so I could cry in peace. The house was empty, but it became my sanctuary. Kicking William out of my heart was like kicking a drug habit. I had no idea what power he had over my emotions until he was suddenly taken from me. In reality I had pushed him away. I was good at pushing people away that cared about me. It was easier to hurt them before they could hurt me.

I sunk to the floor of the shower and pulled my knees to my chest as I let myself get lost in my own sadness. I could have been closer to Judy if I had just tried harder. I never made an effort.

I dried and dressed, not bothering to brush the wet tangles from my hair. I grabbed another book from my room and made my way to the living room. I forced myself to escape into the story of a brooding vampire who falls in love with the helpless and naïve girl.

Day drifted into night and soon I was curled on the couch, alone, with a bottle of vodka beside me.

Tonight, in my dreams, William was in my arms.

I held him close to me as he stroked my hair and told me how much he loved me. I smiled and told him how much he meant to me. A small delicate hand snaked over his shoulder from behind as Angela's face appeared.

"I thought you loved me?" she pouted. William turned back to face in and kissed her deeply.

"Of course I love you, Angela." Their eyes both fell on me as the laughed.

I sat up, heart racing, as I felt along the floor for my bottle. I knocked it over and quickly wrapped my hands around the neck of it. I unscrewed the cap and drank back the contents until it ran dry.

I let myself fall back on the couch and waited for my heartbeat to slow so I could go back to my heart wrenching nightmares.

They did not disappoint.

William appeared with his hands and mouth all over a woman. His back was to me. I ran to him, crying, begging him to stop. As I grabbed his arm and turned his body, I was face to face with my aunt.

I sat up, drenched in sweat once again as the sunlight streaming through the blinds made my head to pound.

Teresa Mummert

At least it was morning. I could use a few hours without the pain of seeing William.

I decided to venture out of the house today. I needed to get away. Some social interaction would do me some good. I made my way to the local grocery store and stocked up on a few can goods, just in case my appetite ever resurfaced. I also grabbed a variety of liquors. I was willing to try anything to help dull the ache in my heart.

By the time I returned to my aunt's house, I had successfully killed two hours of the day. It was awful. I prayed for the days to pass and when night came, I begged for the sun to rise and the nightmares to end.

William hadn't tried to contact me since our last conversation. He was obviously fine without me. Why couldn't I get over him? Why did his moving on make it so much harder?

201

I sat my bags on the counter, prepared a can of chicken noodle soup, and made myself an icepack. The alcohol was numbing the pain less and less, and soon I would have to go to greater measures to remove William from my heart. Perhaps replace the aching emptiness with someone else. It didn't matter who. Anyone who could make me feel like I was alive again would do. I shook the thought from my mind and drank down my drink. The thought of being in someone else's arms made me sick.

The microwave dinged and I grabbed my steaming hot food. I sat at the table and took a few bites. Nothing tasted good anymore. I got no joy out of life.

I was a basket case before William, but how did I let it get to this point? Because he gave me hope. When I felt like I had nothing, was worth nothing, he made me feel like I was special.

I fixed myself another drink and prepared to forget about him. My phone chirped to life. I grabbed it from the table as I checked my messages. It was William.

Can I see you?

I wanted that more than anything. I wanted to hold him, tell him I loved him. I needed him. I couldn't give in now. The hurt and agony I had felt when I saw him with that other woman was too much. Finding out about my aunt.

No.

That was all I said. I switched my phone to silent and stuck it in the silverware drawer. I wasn't sure the point of that, but I was already feeling less pain from my drink and I just wanted to forget.

I walked back the hall and grabbed a new book. This was a dystopian favorite and was sure to take my mind off love lost.

I settled into the couch and began to read. My eyes flicked to the kitchen drawer. I wondered if he had said anything back. If he cared. Maybe he was bored or… lonely. If he was lonely, I'm sure he could find comfort elsewhere. The thought caused my heart to clench. I concentrated on the words on the page. I needed to get lost in the story.

Page after page, I read and willed my mind to drift off in a fantasy. Soon, exhaustion took over and I was able to drift away.

Chapter Twenty-Three

I snuggled tighter into the couch as I fought off another nightmare. This one was William with another woman and tears poured down my face as I begged him to stay with me. He only laughed and turned back to her. To Allison, as he kissed her passionately.

A hand gripped my shoulder firmly and I flipped over, nearly jumping off the couch.

"It's me." William's eyes searched mine as he waited for me to become fully awake.

"Jesus." I let my head fall back against the cushion.

"What was your nightmare about?"

I looked away from his eyes and rubbed my face with both hands.

"Me," he sighed, and rubbed my shoulder with his thumb.

"What are you doing here? How did you... you remember?"

"No. I couldn't take not seeing you. My place feels so empty."

"How did you find me?" I sat up, stretching my achy muscles. The couch was far from comfortable, but I couldn't bring myself to sleep in my bed. Not with the memories of William and I in there.

"There was a tracking app on my phone," he smirked, but his expression quickly went blank. "That probably isn't a good thing." He shook his head and pulled his hand back.

"Not really." I sighed and swung my legs over the edge of the couch.

"I really fucked up." It wasn't a question and I didn't respond. He swallowed hard and shoved his hands in his front pockets.

"How did you get here?" I asked, remembering his car had been totaled in the accident.

"I took a cab." I nodded and pushed myself up to stand in front of him. The electricity in the air was palpable. I pulled my t-shirt down to cover my panties and slid past him. He followed me into the kitchen, sitting down at the table.

I began to make a pot of coffee, knowing damn well I wouldn't be going back to sleep now. I glanced at the clock on the stove. It was a quarter past four.

"Whose funeral did we attend?"

My body went stiff as I held onto the counter. I cleared my throat.

"My aunt's." I tried to keep my voice from shaking as I turned around. "You remember?"

"Not everything. Just bits and pieces." I turned back to the counter and finished preparing the coffee.

"Did she live here? With you?" he asked as I sat a mug down in front of him. "Thank you."

"I lived here with her, yes." I glanced towards the hallway and took a small sip of my drink. He looked behind him, following my eyes.

"It has to be hard for you to be here." He took a drink and I nodded. He had no idea.

"You can come home... with me. I won't touch you if that's what you want. I can sleep on the couch. I haven't been able to sleep since you left."

I held up my hand to stop him from talking. "I couldn't make you sleep on the couch in your own home."

"Then it's settled. We'll sleep together. Strictly sleep, I meant." He grinned playfully and I couldn't stop the smile from spreading across my face. Why did he have to be so damn sweet all of the sudden? It was hard to say no to those big blue eyes. So easy to forget all the hurt.

"Please, Emma. I need you." He reached across the table and placed his hand on mine. He was suffering with loneliness as much as I was, just not the heartbreak. I envied his memory loss.

There was no way I could tell him no. I bit my lip and nodded. He flew out of his chair and wrapped his hands around my waist, lifting me off the ground and spinning me. I squeezed his neck tightly and inhaled his scent. He smelled of soap and musky cologne. Unmistakably William.

"Grab your things. I want to get you home." The way he said home made my heart race.

He sat me down and I took a second to regain my balance after he had made me dizzy.

I dashed back the hallway and began throwing some of my clothes in a bag. I didn't want to take too much time and talk myself out of going. He needed me I told myself. I couldn't leave him helpless and alone. I laughed at the thought of William ever being helpless. It was me who needed him.

"What's so funny?"

I jumped and turned to see William in the doorway of my bedroom. The memories of us in this room together flooded my mind and every part of my body noticed. He pushed off the frame and walked towards me, smiling. His eyes glanced around the unfamiliar room.

"I'm ready." I slung the bag onto my shoulder. He reached out, letting his fingertips graze my skin as he slid the strap of my bag off my shoulder. Every nerve in body took notice.

"I'll carry this for you." He reached out his hand for me. I hesitated but placed my hand in his. He laced our fingers together and pulled me down the hall.

Chapter Twenty-Four

I gripped the steering wheel tightly causing my knuckles to turn white. I could feel William's eyes on me, but couldn't bring myself to look at him. What was I thinking? How long could I live in this fantasy with him before he got his memory back and it all came crashing down?

I reached out and turned on the radio, relaxing as the music drowned out my thoughts. Listening to the lyrics of *Criminal*, I had to laugh to myself. At least William wasn't a criminal. William's eyes were on me again and I cleared my throat and switched the station.

I didn't loosen my grip on the steering wheel until we pulled inside the garage of William's place. His eyes lingered on me for another minute before he got out of the car. I blew out a loud breath and opened my door to follow him. He grabbed my bag from the backseat of my beat up Rabbit and slung it over his shoulder.

I followed him up the stairs and waited as he unlocked the door. He swung it wide open and waited for me to walk inside. It felt like home. I missed being here with him. It was the only place in the world I wanted to be. I stopped a few feet inside the door and stretched as I yawned.

"Want to go to bed?" His breath tickled my ear from behind me.

I was suddenly nervous to be in his bed with him. I knew it was only a matter of time before I gave into my carnal wants. I missed his hands on my body, possessively claiming me as his. I missed feeling anything else besides sadness.

"Come." He walked around me and held out his and for mine. That word coming from his lips was enough to make me lose all of my senses. Did he really have no idea what kind of effect he had on me? Maybe this was just another horrible nightmare. Soon enough he would break my heart and I would awake on my aunt's couch.

I slipped my fingers in his and he smiled as I trailed behind him to his bedroom. It was clean and smelled of laundry soap. I looked around, letting my eyes come to rest on the large bed in the center of the room. His eyes stayed pinned to me as he slipped off his shirt and began to unbuckle his belt.

"Maybe I should take the couch." I turned towards the door willing myself to leave the room. Two strong arms wrapped themselves around my waist and he pulled me back against his body. The length of him pressed firmly against my bottom. He let out a small groan at the contact. The high of having him against me took over.

"Please don't leave me." His lips grazed my ear. I let my eyes fall closed. "Whatever you want from me... whatever you need from me I will give it to you, just please don't leave me."

"I want... I need... time." I breathed as his breath tickled my neck. He reluctantly took a step back and let his arms fall to his sides. I took a deep breath and turned back to him. Our eyes locked and I wanted to be strong and run the other way but I just couldn't. My hands went to my waist and I undid the button of my jeans. I wiggled my hips as I slipped them down my legs and kicked them off onto the floor.

William did the same as he watched me cautiously. I turned and slipped under the covers of the bed. After a moment, William did the same, careful not to touch me. I hated this. I hated the distance between us. It felt like we were a million miles apart. I knew it would be selfish of me to take advantage of him when he had no idea what had happened between us. Once his memory returned he would be the man who had lied to me and used me. He would be the man I had hated.

He wasn't that man now. Right now, he just wanted to be near me. He may not remember us, but he knew we had something important. Right now, I needed that connection more than anything else. I reached below the covers and grabbed the hem of my shirt, dragging it over my head and tossing it on the floor.

William's breath hitched and his fingers slowly slid across my hip. He pulled me toward him, making me to fall onto my back. He was on his side, hovering over me, his hand now cupping my jaw. My body was shaking. I wanted him. Needed him, but it had to be on my terms.

His minty breath blew into my mouth as we stared at each other for what felt like an eternity. I pushed back on his shoulder and he lay back as I slipped a leg over his waist. He stilled, afraid to touch me. Afraid I would run if he did something wrong. His confidence had left with his memories.

I tugged on his boxers and slid them down his legs, scratching him with my nails down his thighs. He was impossibly hard. I hovered over his waist as his hands came up to rub over my hipbones.

"I need you, Emma. Please…" His fingers slipped into the small scrap of fabric of my underwear, along my inner thigh.

"Ahhh…" I panted as he licked his lips.

I felt incredibly powerful and I understood why he enjoyed being in control.

"Rip them." He looked up at me to see if he had heard me correctly. "Rip them off me." I was panting. He looped his fingers in the fabric and gave a quick tug. They fell away from my body and he tossed them on the floor. I grabbed both of his hands and fell forward, pinning them next to his head. My mouth hovered over his as I let my hips drop, grazing his length with my wetness. We moaned together at the touch. I rotated my hips once more and he lifted his to increase the pressure.

"I want to touch you," he groaned, and he lifted his hips to meet mine again. I shook my head.

I captured his bottom lip between my teeth and gave a gentle tug.

"Fuck," he moaned, pushing against my hands.

"Bad boy," I warned and pushed back against him. I slid myself against his length. I felt so powerful. It was amazing. All of the hurt, the pain that I had felt was replaced with lust. I licked his upper lip and his head came off the bed, capturing my lips in his. I let them fall open and he slipped his tongue inside, deepening our kiss. His hips lifted and I moaned into his mouth.

"Do you enjoy teasing me?" His tongue plunged back into my mouth. I had enjoyed it, but I enjoy this William more. The strong and aggressive man who knows exactly what I need. I needed to forget. I need to feel nothing but him.

"You don't like it?" I was panting.

"I'll take you any way I can get you."

In one quick motion, he entered me. My back arched in pleasure as a small whimper escaped my lips. I hadn't realized how empty I was without him until I finally had him again. I widened my legs, granting him deeper access. I let my head fall to the side as I panted, getting lost in the moment. I moved my hips in perfect synchronicity with his.

"God... I love you." As the words left my mouth, his body suddenly stilled. I froze, terrified to look him in the eyes.

"You love me?"

I knew it was a stupid thing to say to a man who had no idea who I was. To him, this was just a casual fling. One of many he has had in his life, I am sure. Pain stabbed at my heart. I'm sure he was regretting bringing this stranger into his bed, no matter how drawn to me he felt.

"Look at me." He wasn't commanding like the William I knew. His voice was shaky. I slowly turned my head to look him in the eye. He stared at me quietly before his hips slowly began to rock into me. My body picked up where it had left off, my orgasm building deep inside of me as I stared into William's eyes from above him.

Every emotion I had felt for him washed over me as my release finally came. He never became rough of forced me to do anything. It was exactly what I needed. I slid off his body and lay back on the mattress.

I turned on my side as his arms wrapped around me from behind and he trailed tiny kisses over my shoulder. My body shook against his as I cried silently to myself. His grip tightened but he did not say a word. He held me until I fell asleep in his arms.

I really was alone now. Even with William's arms wrapped around me. He had no recollection of what he put me through, the loss I suffered before our accident. I felt empty and broken.

Chapter Twenty-Five

The next morning the smell of coffee surrounded me. I woke from a nightmare free night. At least his unknowing arms still offered me comfort. I stretched and slipped out of bed. I found my suitcase at the far side of his room and dug through it for a pair of underwear. All of my clothes had been washed and folded neatly back in the case. I was grateful considering William was making it a habit to rip apart my underwear. I would have to go shopping soon.

I got dressed and quietly tiptoed out into the expansive living area. I sat down at the island. William was leaning over the far counter, his back to me as he bent over, his hands in his dark hair. I wanted to run to him, to wrap my arms around him, but I couldn't. I should have never slept with him last night. It was only a band-aid over our problems. They ran far too deep. My hand made a noise as I brought it down on the counter and William's head shot up, realizing he was no longer alone.

"Sorry." I tucked my hair behind my ear. He rolled his head from side to side, stretching his neck before grabbing the pot of coffee and filling two mugs.

He sat a steaming mug down in front of me, turning to dig some milk out of the fridge. I poured a heavy helping of sugar into my cup and he topped it off with a splash of milk.

"Thank you," I whispered and took a small sip. William didn't join me. He stayed on the far side of the counter, spinning the container of sugar over the surface. I blushed as I watched it in his hands, remembering a very fun morning with him on this very counter.

When I looked up his eyes where already on mine as he watched me.

"Do you... remember anything new?" I held my breath as he stared for another moment.

"I wish I did." His eyes dropped back to the sugar before he released it and took a long drink from his mug. I nodded and focused on my cup, praying my pink cheeks would fade back to normal. I couldn't allow my heart to be his without knowing the truth. At this rate, I wasn't sure he would ever remember.

"Hungry?" William had turned to the fridge, and was pulling out breakfast foods. I shrugged my shoulders.

My appetite was still not making an appearance. I was too stressed out. "I think I'll skip breakfast."

He didn't say anything. He began cracking eggs into a dish, adding a splash of milk and a few spices. As his pan heated, he diced up some lunchmeat and mozzarella to add to the concoction. I watched his muscles flex and pull in his back as he worked. I followed the lines of his tribal tattoo that wrapped up his arm and over his shoulder, disappearing over his chest.

I don't know how long I was staring. Lost in the thought of him. He turned and placed to plates down on the counter. It smelled phenomenal, but my stomach was still in knots.

"I don't think I can." I placed a hand over my stomach as it filled with butterflies. He rounded the island and took a seat next to mine. His arm brushed against mine.

"You need to eat something." He cut his food and placed a bite in his mouth.

"I'm fine, really." I smiled politely and his face went expressionless.

"Eat."

I guess some things never change. I picked up my fork and speared a small bite of eggs, blowing on it before sticking it in my mouth.

"Thanks." I shot him an appreciative smile. He smiled back and continued to devour his breakfast.

When we finished eating, he stood to take our plates. I placed my hand on his wrists to stop him.

"Why don't you let me get that?" I stood and grabbed the plates from his hands. I needed something to distract me. Anything to take my mind off him. I knew last night was a horrible mistake. It would be twice as hard to walk away when he begins to remember.

William's hands snaked around my waist as I scrubbed our plates. I let my eyes fall closed for a second as he nuzzled into my neck.

"William..."

"Shh…" His lips brushed against my throat.

"I don't think we should do this." I struggled to keep my breath even but my heart was already racing.

"Don't think." His hand slipped to the waistband of my panties. His fingers dipping under the edge of the thin fabric.

"I can't."

All of the air left the room as William's body stilled behind me. I opened my eyes as he backed away from my body. I turned to face him. He was running his hands through his hair and letting out a deep breath.

"What's the problem?" His hands stretched out in front of him. I backed myself against the sink as I struggled not to run into his arms.

"You don't remember…You don't…" Tears filled my eyes as I swallowed the lump in my throat.

He stepped closer, filling the gap between us. His hands rubbed against my cheek.

"It doesn't matter. Whatever happened doesn't matter now. We are here. We both want to be with each other. Why fight it?" His thumb stroked the corner of my eye and I let them fall closed, bathing in his touch.

"I may not know what I did to hurt you so badly, but I know that we once loved each other. I know you still love me or you wouldn't be here right now. I know it hurts you to be with me, but you are willing to suffer through the pain to be by my side." His body moved closer until he was touching every part of me.

"I know I love you, too. I can feel it." He took my and held it tightly on his chest. His heart was beating out of control.

"Give me a chance to make this right. I will do anything to make this right."

My tears began to fall at his confession. My heart couldn't take any more. I pushed my lips hard against his as his free hand slipped into my hair and held me firmly against him.

"I'm sorry," He whispered into my mouth. "Start over with me. We can make new memories. I'll be whoever you need me to be."

I threw my arms around him and squeezed him as tightly as I could. I wanted that. More than anything. I needed that. I needed him.

Chapter Twenty-Six

After all we had been through; I wanted to do something carefree and fun. I took William to see a new movie I had been dying to see. It was a romantic comedy and I knew he wasn't enjoying it. He didn't complain though. He sat beside me, holding my hand and chuckling softly. It was nice being out and acting as if we were a normal couple.

I even began to believe it over dinner as we sat in booth in the middle of a nearly empty restaurant. I was nervous we would run into someone we knew, but William stroked the back of my hand and assured me that none of that mattered to him. He was willing to give up everything if it made me happy.

I didn't want that. He would one day resent me for taking away something he loved. It would be selfish. Still, I let my mind entertain the idea.

He even remembered what foods he liked and disliked when he read over the menu. I was excited for his progress but terrified that all of this would come crashing down soon.

"What's wrong?" His voice was wrought with concern. I smiled weakly.

"It's nothing." I glanced down at the menu and tried to keep the mood light.

"Please, just tell me what is bothering you so I can make it right."

I laced my fingers in his. Just as I opened my mouth to speak a young woman, around my age approached the table.

"Hey, Mr. Honor!" She was bubbly and cheery. I pulled my hand back quickly and placed it on my lap. I didn't recognize her. She must have been in his class during a different period. Her eyes shot back between us. William nodded and smiled and the girl continued on her way.

"Who was that?" I asked, leaning in and keeping my voice at barely a whisper.

"I have no idea." He cocked his eyebrow and I broke out in a spontaneous giggle fit. Of course he didn't know.

"She is probably one of your students." I waited for him to process that information.

"I'm a teacher?" he laughed at the idea.

"A professor at Kippling College."

"Were you one of my…" He raised an eyebrow, struggling to regain the memories of his life.

I nodded but didn't elaborate. I'm sure it was becoming obvious that our relationship was less than traditional.

Our meal went well without any other close calls. I made sure to keep my hands on my side of the table, fighting the urge to touch him.

William begged me to give him the keys to drive us back to his place, but I stood firm.

"You don't even know how to get home!" I joked.

"Two lefts and straight through to Riverton Street." His face was unreadable.

My breath caught in my throat.

"Me?" I could barely push out the word. He shook his head and looked down at the ground. I sighed and watched him open the passenger side door, slipping in. I relaxed and joined him inside the car. I immediately cranked the volume on the radio. All of this was so overwhelming.

A faint ringing sounded, barely audible over the music. I glanced at William as he slipped his phone from his pocket. He glanced at the screen and slipped it back into his pocket.

"Who was that?" I asked. I didn't care if my voice was laced with jealousy.

"I don't know." He shrugged and looked out the passenger window. Rage flew through me as I whipped the car to the shoulder of the road and slammed it into park.

"You knew enough not to answer it. Who was it?" My heart was pounding out of my chest. Of course William's past wouldn't just melt away with his memories.

"Someone named Allison."

My heart seized in my chest. It felt like someone had punched me hard in the stomach and I literally doubled over in pain.

"You… remember her?" I was on the verge of passing out and my heart pounded like a drum in my ears.

"No. She called while you were gone. I had no idea who she was… at first." His hands reached for mine and I pulled back, disgusted. "I don't remember her. I only have what she said to go by."

I turned back to the steering wheel and let my head rest against it.

"Please." His voice cracked as he spoke.

I put the car in drive and headed toward his place, not bothering to adhere to the speed limit. I didn't care what happened to me any longer. I was dying inside. Dying for him. I needed to make the pain go away. I knew he could do that for me even if he didn't remember how.

When we made it to his place, I barely waited for the car to stop before jumping out and slamming the door. I hated him. I hated the way I felt, but I couldn't run away.

He followed me up the stairs. I unlocked the door and pushed it open, going inside and waiting for him. He looked sad and for a moment, I felt sorry for him. That feeling was quickly washed away as his phone rang again. I shoved him hard against the wall next to the door. I pushed it closed with my elbow.

My hands quickly worked to undo the buckle of his belt as he stared at me, not sure if it was okay to touch me. I wanted to make him remember, or, at the very least, make myself forget. I pulled down his zipper and freed him from his boxers. He reached for me, his fingers trailing down my arm. I pushed it away. He groaned as my fingers wrapped around him and his body twitched beneath my grip.

"Emma, please..."

I placed my finger over his lips to keep him from talking. I didn't want to fight or talk things out. I just wanted to be lost in pleasure. I sank to my knees and took him in my mouth.

"Ahh…" His fingers tangled in my hair. I pulled back, using my teeth to scratch his length. "Fuck, Emma." His head fell back against the wall as I circled my tongue around him, pushing him deeper into my throat. "I want you," he moaned.

I bit lightly, warning him to stop talking. His hands fisted, pulling my hair at the nape of my neck. I opened my mouth and waited for his hands to relax. They did and I rewarded him by licking his length. As another quiet moan escaped him, I backed away and rose to my feet. His mouth hung open as he struggled to regain his composure. I turned and walked to the bedroom. His eyes followed me and eventually so did he.

I stood at the foot of the bed.

"In here I'm in charge." I cleared my throat and tried to sound confident. "You don't touch me unless I tell you it's okay." He walked closer, but stopped short. I grabbed his belt and slid it out of his belt loops. "Take your clothes off."

Teresa Mummert

Chapter Twenty-Seven

I watched him pull his shirt over his head, the muscles of his stomach flexing as he moved. He slipped his jeans over his hips and kicked them to the side. I looked to his boxers and back to his eyes. He swallowed hard and shoved them down. His hand immediately wrapped around his shaft.

"I didn't tell you to touch yourself."

His hand reluctantly moved and he clenched his fist.

"Lay down." I motioned towards the bed with my head.

He crawled to the center of the bed and waited for me. I pulled my shirt over my head as his eyes danced over my body. My body was still shaking with anger. I slipped my jeans and underwear over my hips together and kicked them off my feet. I reluctantly looked back up to William, clutching the belt in my hand. No point in stopping now.

I climbed up the bed, forcing him to lie down beneath me.

"Put your hands above your head." My voice cracked and I silently scolded myself. "Now!" I shouted with much more confidence. He lifted his hands above him and I smiled. It worked. I took the belt and looped it over his wrists and through a slat in his headboard. He tugged at the restraints. I raked my nails down his chest, watching his muscles jump under my fingers. He licked his lips as he lifted his hips into me. My eyes fell closed, losing myself in the sensation. "No," my voice was small and I had to swallow hard to fight back the moan that threatened to escape my lips. "Don't move." I smacked him hard on the chest. His jaw clenched, but his hips dropped back to the mattress. My teeth dug into my lower lip and

Teresa Mummert

I reached between us, grabbing him firmly in my hands.

I pushed him against me as I slowly slid my body down over him. He was rock hard and obviously enjoyed being dominated just as much as he enjoyed doing it to others. I rocked my hips against him as I let my hands wander over my chest, pinching my nipples into hard peaks. William groaned as he watched me, pulling on the belt to free himself. I turned my attention back to him. I ran my finger down over his mouth. He kissed against my finger, flicking it quickly with his tongue. I let my eyes fall closed, not able to stare into his eyes without being overrun by sadness. A lump formed in my throat. I let my hands slide to his shoulders, gripping him painfully tight until wetness coated my fingertips. Panic soon overtook my sadness as I opened my eyes. Smears of blood dotted his perfect body.

"I-I'm sorry." My hips stilled.

"Don't stop." He pushed himself deeper inside of me, not fazed by the pain. I matched his movement, coming down harder on him, twisting my hips to rub myself against his pubic bone. He growled and my body began to twitch around him. My body trembled as we both reached the peak of our pleasure. I collapsed onto his chest and reached above his head, freeing his hands.

As soon as he was unbound, his arms wrapped around my body. He pulled me tightly into his chest, cradling me.

"I'm sorry I hurt you," I whispered as I gently stroked the nail marks on his shoulder.

"I've obviously hurt you far worse. I deserve whatever you give me." He squeezed me into him and kissed the top of my head.

It was unlike William to be so caring. I knew he had loved me but I had never seen this side of him. The accident didn't magically make him into a new person. This was a part of him that had always been there. It was comforting. I needed this from him now more than ever.

"Emma." He waited for me to respond. I turned my head to face him. "Tell me about you."

I sighed and buried my head back into his chest. "What do you want to know?" I tensed in his arms.

"Everything."

"I am an only child. I grew up in Michigan. I came to live with my aunt a few years ago when..." I was giving him the cliff's notes version of events. I didn't like bringing up the horrible things in my life that I couldn't change.

"What?" he coaxed me to continue.

"When my parents died in a car accident."

His body went rigid and his breathing grew heavier.

"A car accident?" he asked as if he misunderstood. I nodded against him. "Fuck, Emma. You must have been so scared when I..." I knew exactly what he was thinking.

"It wasn't your fault. It was an accident."

"I could have killed us both." He swallowed hard and I felt his heart rate pick up in his chest, thudding against my ear.

"You remember..."

He shook his head and his grip tightened around me and I could barely breathe but I didn't pull away. Tears began spilling from my eyes onto his chest. "That's why you hate me..." His voice trailed off.

"I don't hate you, William. We were fighting before the crash."

He pulled my chin up to look him in the eye. His eyebrows pulled together.

"What happened to us?" I could hear the fear in sadness in his voice. I wanted to tell him everything but I wasn't sure I could stay after everything was out in the open. I needed William. Even if he didn't know who I was. He was all I had left in the world.

"It was nothing." I tried to look down but he kept his fingers firm under my chin.

"I want to know. I want you to tell me." His eyes narrowed and I knew he wouldn't be satisfied until he had an answer. I was panicking. This was the end. I was going to lose him forever. I wouldn't get to make the decision as to whether or not I was strong enough to stay and stick things out. It was all going to come crashing down now whether I liked it or not.

"Tell me."

"You asked me to marry you. I told you no." I paused waiting to see if he believed what I was saying. It was the truth, just not the cause for the fight before the accident.

"You said no." He looked down between us, sadness in his eyes.

"I was scared you would regret it if you lost your job. You love teaching. I could never live with myself if you lost that."

His eyes met mine again.

"I wouldn't have asked if I didn't love you more. You are more important than some job. How could you think otherwise?" He looked genuinely offended. Great. This went better the first time around.

My mind flashed to my father, angry and unhappy. His job was his life, not his family. He worked hard every day to provide for us. When he would come home, my mother would fight with him about not being around enough. Life was miserable. I didn't want to be that to William.

William took my hand and placed it against his chest. His heart hammered against my fingers as he looked deep into my eyes.

"Emma, I don't know what happened between us and I don't care. My heart races out of control every time you come near me. I'm terrified that you will walk out of that door and it will stop. I can't live without you. I don't care if I never remember my life. I want to start a new one... with you."

I swallowed hard as I studied his face. "Yes... let's do it. Let's get married."

His lips crashed into mine.

Chapter Twenty-Eight

"Are you ready?" William laced his fingers in mine and squeezed them tightly. I swallowed hard taking several deep breaths.

"Yes," I whispered. I was terrified, but I knew I was one hundred percent in love with William. I tried living without him. Those days without him were the hardest days of my life. I needed him.

Stephen stepped towards us, a small stack of papers in his hands. He was smiling as he looked at William.

"Emma," The mayor greeted me, inclining his head.

"Good to see you again." I was giggling like a schoolgirl.

William nodded at his old friend as he took my hand in his.

"We are here today to participate in a most joyous occasion, to celebrate one of life's greatest moments, by acknowledging the wedding of William and Emma. William, do you take Emma to be your lawfully wedded wife? Do you promise to love, honor, and protect her? Share the good times and achievements as well as the hard times and disappointments? Keep her in sickness and in sorrow and to be faithful to her forevermore?"

William smiled as he looked into my eyes.

"I do."

"Emma, do you take William to be your lawfully wedded husband? Do you promise to love, honor, and protect him? Share the good times and achievements as well as the hard times and disappointments? Keep him in sickness and in sorrow and to be faithful to him forevermore?"

"I do."

William looked to Stephen, who nodded for him to recite his portion of the vows.

"I give you this ring in token and pledge as a symbol of all that we share with my constant faith and abiding love." He slipped a small silver band with a princess cut diamond onto my fingers.

"Now that you have joined yourselves in matrimony, may you strive always to meet this commitment with the same spirit you now exhibit. We all bear witness to this ceremony you have just performed, and you may now call yourselves by those old and respected names, husband and wife. May God bless this union. You may kiss the bride."

William's arms wrapped around my waist as he pulled me into him. His lips feverishly kissed mine.

"I love you," I whispered against his lips. His lips curled into a smile against mine.

"I love you, Emma Honor. Now you are mine forever."

~The End~

About The Author

I was a Russian spy at the ripe age of thirteen, given my uncanny ability to tell if someone was lying (I also read fortunes on the weekends). By sixteen I had become too much of a handful for the Lethal Intelligence Ensemble (L.I.E.). I was quickly exiled to the south of France were I worked with wayward elephants in the Circus of Roaming Animals and People (C.R.A.P.). I was able to make ends meet by selling my organs on the black market for pocket change and beer money. At the age of twenty-three I decided to expand my horizons and become a blackjack dealer in Ireland. I loved the family atmosphere at Barney's Underground Liquor Lounge (B.U.L.L.). People couldn't resist the allure of Liquor up front and poker in the rear. Eventually, I became tired of the rear and headed off to the United States to try my

252

hand at tall tales. That is what brings us hear today. If you have a moment, I'd like to tell you a story.

(This bio is not to be taken seriously under any circumstance.)

Teresa Mummert is an army wife and mother whose passion in life is writing. Born in Pennsylvania, she lived a small town life before following her husband's military career to Louisiana and Georgia. She has published the Undying Love Vampire Series, Honor Series, and Breaking Sin. She also contributes to SocialSex.Org. Check out her website for samples and updates!

http://www.TeresaMummert.com